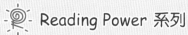

Reading Power 系列

Advanced

閱讀經典文學時光之旅：英國篇

附解析本

宋美璍・編著

三民書局

國家圖書館出版品預行編目資料

閱讀經典文學時光之旅：英國篇／宋美璍編著.－
－初版一刷.－－臺北市: 三民, 2019
面；　　公分.－－(Reading Power系列)

ISBN 978–957–14–6615–6　　(平裝)
1. 英國文學 2. 文學評論

873.2　　　　　　　　　　　　　　108004553

© 　閱讀經典文學時光之旅：英國篇

編 著 者	宋美璍
責任編輯	劉倩茹　曾頌伶
美術編輯	王立涵
內頁繪圖	江正一
發 行 人	劉振強
著作財產權人	三民書局股份有限公司
發 行 所	三民書局股份有限公司
	地址　臺北市復興北路386號
	電話　(02)25006600
	郵撥帳號　0009998–5
門 市 部	(復北店)臺北市復興北路386號
	(重南店)臺北市重慶南路一段61號
出版日期	初版一刷　2019年5月
編　　號	S 807150

行政院新聞局登記證局版臺業字第○二○○號

有著作權‧不准侵害

ISBN　978–957–14–6615–6　　(平裝)

http://www.sanmin.com.tw　三民網路書店
※本書如有缺頁、破損或裝訂錯誤，請寄回本公司更換。

序言

　　本書收錄八篇英國文學的經典作品，有史詩、散文、悲劇和小說，時間貫穿將近一千年。取名《閱讀經典文學時光之旅：英國篇》，強調文學由時光歲月的沉澱所醞釀而成，提振心志、熏陶靈魂的人性馨香。本書內容依寫作年代先後，呈現古英文時期、文藝復興時期、十八世紀末和十九世紀中葉等不同時期，反映作家的所思所慮，以及所處時代的價值觀。這些傳世之作可以說是大時代與傑出創作才思所碰撞出來的智慧火花。

　　這本書歷經多時籌劃、構思與執筆寫作，造就一本文圖並美的文學導讀讀本，適合高中以上學子補充閱讀，並且進行師生互動。選文的考量貼合教育部所頒布的議題，包括海洋教育、法治教育、品德教育、生命教育、家庭教育、科技教育、人權教育和性別教育。議題與文學讀本之間的連結，還有待讀者閱讀過後細細品味。

　　這八項議題的內涵都與人生息息相關，透過文本引出議題的深層意涵，以此提升讀者面對問題時的分析與解決能力，同時也有助於核心素養的發展與深化。《貝奧武夫》談英國先祖英勇駕馭汪洋黑海的凶險和英雄的才德；《烏托邦》講文藝復興時期人本思想初萌之時關乎法治的思辨；《浮士德》在呈現「自作孽」的悲劇後果，提振基督徒的品德與信仰之時，卻也悄然肯定了當代初萌對人本自主的渴望；《哈姆雷特》描述性格與責任義務之間的衝突，由此而生對生命意義的探索；《傲慢與偏見》揉合自傳與虛構，肯定家庭教育的重要，以樂觀浪漫的手法，賦予二位女主角圓滿的結局；《科學怪人》談科技之濫用，是經典的哥德式科幻小說；《孤雛淚》充斥著狄更斯的人道情懷與撻伐人性黑暗面的勇氣，以小說手法呈現真實的社會困境，伸張被欺壓者的人權；《簡愛》讚揚一位獨立的弱勢女性如何自立自強，終能成就自我並且嫁給所愛的男子，達到真正的性別平等。

　　文學關懷人生，書寫人生的種種情境。不論喜怒哀樂或成功失敗，文學家總是透過想像力的渲染，使得筆下的人生成為真實人生的映照，聚焦失敗的憂戚和成功的榮光。

　　讀經典文學的最大收穫是欣賞大作家的文采與巧妙布局，更重要的是他們悲天憫人的胸懷。莎士比亞被歌頌為「具備一個最為寬闊的靈魂」(a most comprehensive soul)，舉世的讀者雖處不同的時代，都能在閱讀他的故事和人物之際發現自我，得到共鳴。經典文學的魔力穿越時空，對接人性的奧微之處。本書的出版希望能夠引起讀者探索複雜的人性，超越自己心智與經驗的小領域，進入一個年輕心靈尚未涉足的大宇宙，從而擴大自我的視野，勵志思齊，同時善用書中英語教學的設計，得到雙重的收穫。

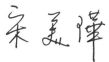

使用說明

關於作者
介紹作者的生平背景、經歷和著作。

年表
條列式列出作者重點生平事件。

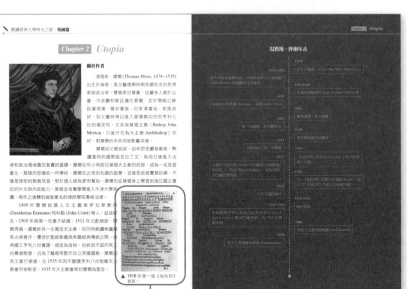

相關資料補充
補充作者、文章相關資料。

朗讀音檔音軌編號
每篇文章有一段完整音檔及三段分段音檔,另有單字朗讀音檔。

Words for Production
Words for Recognition
Idioms and Phrases
精選字彙列表,輔以音標及中譯。

精選字彙
精選文章中重要字彙,並做套色、粗體及註碼等標記。

Something You Should Know
補充說明文章相關小知識。

Discussion
以問題的方式引導讀者思辨文章中的細節。

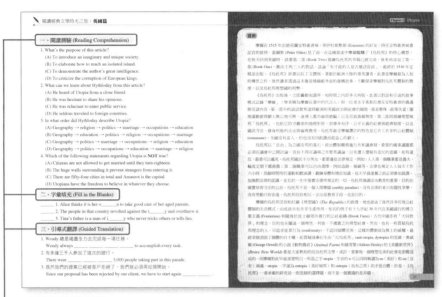

賞析

提供精闢賞析，帶領讀者領略文章中更深層的意義。

課後練習題

題型包含閱讀測驗、字彙填充、引導式翻譯，幫助讀者對於文章閱讀理解與記憶重要的單字。

解析本

提供完整的文章中文翻譯，並附上課後練習題答案與詳盡的試題解析。

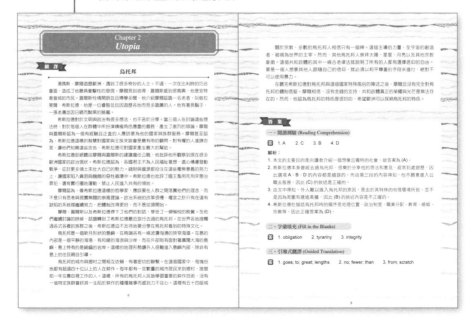

線上音檔下載教學

邊聽邊讀，聽故事學習英文更有趣！
用「聽」的方式，增強你的閱讀力！

STEP 1. 前往「三民東大英文學習網」→「學習素材」→「英語學習素材」下載。
http://www.grandeast.com.tw/englishsite/Mterial?T=263

STEP 2. 進入頁面後，點選想要書籍，進行下載。

閱讀經典文學時光
之旅：英國篇

STEP 3. 下載完成後，會取得一個 zip 檔。

學習素材

英語學習教材

閱讀經典文學時光之旅：英
國篇(內無文字檔，限購買
此書者下載) ｜ 下載

STEP 4. 解壓縮檔案，依據提示輸入指定密碼，即可取得音檔。

請輸入密碼 ✕

請給加密的檔案輸入密碼
C:\Users\user\Desktop\閱讀經典文學時光之旅：...\Track 1-3.mp3
於壓縮檔 閱讀經典文學時光之旅：英國篇.zip

請輸入密碼(E)

☐ 顯示密碼(S)

☐ 適用於所有壓縮檔(A)

整理密碼(O)...

確定 ｜ 取消 ｜ 說明

密碼提示：
Chapter 4 第 8 個單字。

音檔分成完整音檔及分段音
檔兩種模式。檔名按照章節
排列，Track 1、Track 2 等
為完整音檔；Track 1-1、
Track 1-2、Track 1-3 等
為每章節的分段音檔，皆分
三段。讀者可依需求自行選
擇不同音檔下載。
另有單字朗讀音檔！

Track 1　Track 1-1　Track 1-2　Track 1-3

Track 2　Track 2-1　Track 2-2　Track 2-3

Track 3　Track 3-1　Track 3-2　Track 3-3

Track 4　Track 4-1　Track 4-2　Track 4-3

Contents

Chapter 1 *Beowulf*

作者背景與文稿演變過程

　　《貝奧武夫》(*Beowulf*) 的故事描述日耳曼民族英雄貝奧武夫的事跡，時約西元第六世紀初。故事以傳奇的形式代代口傳保存了下來。故事中的人物包括盎格魯─撒克遜 (Anglo-Saxon) 和斯堪地那維亞半島的北歐日耳曼民族，例如丹麥人和基特人，主角在歷史上確有其人，但是故事加入文學的想像，使得故事細節充滿戲劇張力。這些民族在基督教起源之前早已存在，歷史上慣稱為異教徒 (pagans)，其中盎格魯─撒克遜人在第五世紀征服英國之後，大規模移居英國，並受到已經改信基督教的原住民塞爾柱人的同化，成為虔誠的基督徒。這個巨大轉變也反映在《貝奧武夫》的故事敘述中。由於傳到英國時，講故事的人已是一位基督徒，在故事中添加了基督教的信仰和文字用語，使得故事大約在第八到第十世紀之間由某一位識字人士（極可能是教會神職人員）寫成文字稿之後，已然在原來故事的異教價值（個人主義英雄崇拜）之中加入對上帝和基督教義的稱頌。由口述到書寫，由讚嘆個人豪傑到混雜了對上帝為宇宙唯一真神的信仰，這個改變歷時約三百年，吻合盎格魯─撒克遜人占領並逐漸定居英國的過程。因此，後人讀到的《貝奧武夫》的作者已不可考，而文字稿也帶有異教與基督教價值觀夾雜的痕跡。

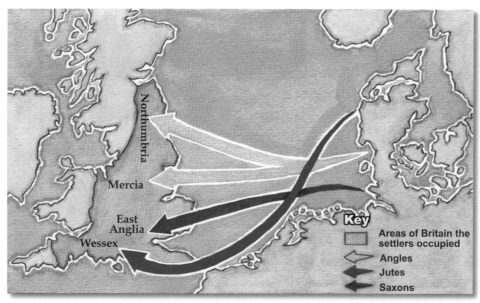

　　▲ 西元第五世紀，盎格魯─撒克遜人征服英國，引發日耳曼其他各族裔西進移居英國。如圖所示，盎格魯人進入中部和北部，撒克遜人進入東南部，基特人則進入西南部。

Beowulf

[PROLOGUE: THE RISE OF THE DANISH NATION]
So. The Spear-Danes in days gone by and the kings who
ruled them had courage and greatness. We have heard of
those princes' heroic campaigns.

There was Shield Sheafson, scourge of many tribes, a
wrecker of mead-benches, rampaging among foes. This terror
of the hall-troops had come far. A foundling to start with, he
would flourish later on as his powers waxed and his worth
was proved. In the end each clan on the outlying coasts
beyond the whale-road had to yield to him and begin to pay
tribute. That was one good king.

Afterward a boy-child was born to Shield, a cub in the
yard, a comfort sent by God to that nation. He knew what
they had tholed, the long times and troubles they'd come
through without a leader; so the Lord of Life, the glorious
Almighty, made this man renowned. Shield had fathered a
famous son: Beow's name was known through the north. And
a young prince must be prudent like that, giving freely while
his father lives so that afterward in age when fighting starts
steadfast companions will stand by him and hold the line.
Behavior that's admired is the path to power among people
everywhere.

Shield was still thriving when his time came and he
crossed over into the Lord's keeping. His warrior band did
what he bade them when he laid down the law among the
Danes: they shouldered him out to the sea's flood, the chief
they revered who had long ruled them.

◀ 現今廣為流傳諾頓版英國文學史 (*Norton Anthology of English Literature*) 中的《貝奧武夫》現代英文選文，是由諾貝爾文學獎得主謝默斯‧希尼 (Seamus Heaney) 所翻譯。

此圖是《貝奧武夫》現在僅存古英文手稿的其中一頁，收藏於大英博物館。古英文為古日耳曼語，與現在所使用的英語，在字母、拼字和文法等各方面都大不相同。 ▶

《貝奧武夫》原手稿是以古日耳曼語西撒克遜方言書寫，經過十多世紀的演變才有今日的現代英文版。二十世紀初之後，這首古詩的讀者才漸漸增加。據文學史專家推測，英國著名文豪莎士比亞 (William Shakespeare)、濟慈 (John Keats) 等人，可能都不知道有這首詩的存在。一直到二十世紀中葉以後，許多當代詩人如奧登 (W. H. Auden)、休斯 (Ted Hughes) 和希尼 (Seamus Heaney) 皆深受此詩啟發。《貝奧武夫》遂逐漸被認為是英國文學的起源，而且被視為經典 (canon)，被英國人用以與希臘羅馬史詩相提並論，代表英國先祖的文學成就。

Beowulf was a **warrior**[1] of great renown throughout the Germanic lands. He had royal blood and was nephew of King Hygelac, the ruler of Geatland. The nobles of that era upheld* the heroic code. In his conduct, Beowulf was a perfect example of the values of life. He was courageous, successful in warfare, loyal to his king, and proud of his deeds.

This mighty warrior was said to have the strength of thirty men. He had built his reputation by defeating numerous enemies of his kingdom in battle. He was particularly famous for a legendary swimming match with another great warrior, his boyhood friend Breca. When they were still youths, they challenged each other to dive into the icy sea with their swords to kill sea monsters. They swam and fought for five days and nights. A monster dragged Beowulf under the water, but he slew it and eight other sea monsters before returning to the shore in triumph.

When Beowulf heard that a terrible monster was attacking the court of Hrothgar, the king of Denmark, he resolved to go to the monarch's aid. Beowulf was ambitious to augment his fame. Moreover, he had a bond of loyalty to the Danish king. Hrothgar had once helped Beowulf's father end a bloody dispute with another tribe by paying them treasure.

Hence, Beowulf sailed with fourteen of his trusted warriors to Denmark. They traveled to the great mead-hall Hrothgar had built. There Hrothgar had established his throne. The mead-hall had **symbolized**[2] the power and prestige of the Danes, yet now it became the focus of the troubles that had fallen on the kingdom. After greeting and paying **tribute**[3] to Hrothgar, Beowulf inquired about the monster.

He was told that an evil creature, known as Grendel, inhabited the swamps and wild countryside surrounding the hall. When Grendel had heard the warriors celebrating and praising God, he became angry. One night he attacked the sleeping warriors in the mead-hall, carrying thirty back to the swamp where he slaughtered them and gorged himself on their flesh. The nightly raids* continued for twelve years and many more warriors were killed. Weapons could not harm the creature and thereafter the Danes had to abandon the mead-hall at night when Grendel roamed.

Beowulf claimed that he could defeat this terrible foe with his bare hands. He boasted about his deeds and his success in killing sea monsters. The Danes were inspired by the **eloquent**[4] speech. Their gloom was replaced by flickers of hope. That night Beowulf and the fourteen Geats stayed in the mead-hall and waited.

Suddenly, they heard the sound of the door being torn away. Grendel burst in. The monster devoured a warrior and then tried to pick up Beowulf. However, Beowulf grabbed the creature's arm and would not let go. Grendel was shocked by the powerful grasp. He attempted to break loose and the two battled around the mead-hall. Finally, Beowulf ended the fight by ripping Grendel's arm off from the shoulder. Grendel was fatally wounded and **staggered**[5] back to the swamp to die.

To prove his victory, Beowulf hung up Grendel's arm from the wall of the mead-hall. Hrothgar and his warriors were amazed to see this trophy and hailed Beowulf as the most **valiant**[6] of all the heroes.

Something You Should Know

　　《貝奧武夫》被學者公認為英國文學史上第一部史詩。史詩是非常古老的文學表達形式，以韻體寫作，講述古代的英雄事蹟，歌頌英雄的膽識與超凡的技能。古希臘詩人荷馬 (Homer) 所著《伊利亞德》(*Iliad*) 和《奧德賽》(*Odyssey*)，以及古羅馬詩人維吉爾 (Virgil) 所著《伊尼亞德》(*Aeneid*)，是最為人知的偉大史詩。史詩歌頌英雄的豐功偉業，也哀悼他們的凋零離世，因此，史詩的語調常見接近哀悼詩。英雄在世時發光發熱，死後受人傳頌，聲名不朽。

單字朗讀 完整 MP3 Ch1 Vocabulary

Words for Production

1. warrior [ˋwɔrɪɚ] *n.* [C]（尤指舊時的）武士，勇士
2. symbolize [ˋsɪmbḷˏaɪz] *v.* 象徵；代表
3. tribute [ˋtrɪbjʊt] *n.* [C][U] 讚揚，稱讚
4. eloquent [ˋɛləkwənt] *adj.* 雄辯的
5. stagger [ˋstægɚ] *v.* 搖晃；蹣跚
6. valiant [ˋvæljənt] *adj.* 英勇的；果敢的

Words for Recognition

* uphold [ʌpˋhold] *v.* 支援，維護
* raid [red] *n.* [C] 突襲，襲擊

Idioms and Phrases

1. dive into sth 跳水 …；下潛 …
2. burst in 突然闖入
3. break loose 擺脫；掙脫
4. hail sb/sth as sth 讚揚…為…

Discussion

Beowulf is a hero both because of his character and physical strength. Do you think the definition of a hero has changed with the passage of time? In our times, what are the qualities of a hero? What makes a person, man or woman, worthy of being recognized as a hero?

King Hrothgar held a special banquet in honor of Beowulf. There he rewarded Beowulf with treasure, weapons and armor. Songs were composed and sung in praise of him. It was a joyous celebration. After years of chaos and suffering, order had been restored to the Danish kingdom. On the night of the feast, the king and his warriors slept in the mead-hall, believing they were at last free from further **peril**[7].

They were totally unaware of a new threat, for Grendel had a mother, another savage monster. Seeing her dying son, she flew into a furious rage. She resolved to seek revenge on those who had deprived* her offspring. While the Danes were sleeping, she crossed the wilderness and broke into the hall. She seized Hrothgar's counselor, Aeschere, and slew him. She then **snatched**[8] Grendel's arm from the wall. The warriors attacked her, but she fled into the darkness, carrying her victim's body and her son's limb.

Hrothgar summoned Beowulf to the mead-hall and pleaded with him to assist his people once more. Beowulf agreed and vowed to find Grendel's mother's home and kill her. Thus, Beowulf and his Geat warriors entered the wilderness. They came to a steep cliff which overlooked a lake of **whirling**[9] water. Thick blood rose up from its depths. They gazed in awe at monstrous creatures such as huge water snakes and gigantic sea dragons swimming in the poisonous waters. On the cliff lay Aeschere's head. They then knew that this was the place where Grendel's mother dwelt.

Beowulf dived into the lake and swam down into its depths. It took him nearly a day to reach the bottom. There he was surrounded by sea monsters. He was grabbed by Grendel's mother and dragged to her court. Beowulf's sword could not harm her, so he desperately **wrestled**[10] with her. He was unable to defeat her and was losing the battle. At the time, the exhausted warrior saw a giant sword hanging on the wall. He seized it and sliced the monster's neck. Blood rushed from the wound and Grendel's mother died. Seeing Grendel's corpse nearby, Beowulf cut off its head and swam back up to the surface with his ghastly* trophy.

When the warriors above saw fresh blood surging in the water, they believed it was Beowulf's. They feared the worst. Yet despair turned to delight when their leader appeared on the surface of the lake **clutching**[11] Grendel's head. The band of warriors returned in triumph to the mead-hall, where they were greeted as heroes by the Danes. Hrothgar richly rewarded Beowulf and held another banquet to honor him and his triumphant men. The Danes and Geats **pledged**[12] loyalty and friendship before Beowulf and his warriors voyaged back to their homeland.

The warriors were welcomed at the hall of Beowulf's uncle, King Hygelac, in Geatland. Beowulf told the court about his adventures in Denmark. He mentioned his **courteous**[13] reception by King Hrothgar. He then vividly described how he overcame Grendel in the great mead-hall and Grendel's mother in the **bleak**[14] lake, thereby saving the Danes and earning their praise. Beowulf then generously gave his king a large portion of the treasure he had received from the grateful Danish king. King Hygelac **heralded**[15] Beowulf as a hero and gave him lands and some of his own treasure.

A few years later, King Hygelac was killed in a battle in a war with the Swedish kingdom. Beowulf inherited the throne and defeated Geatland's enemies. He ruled wisely for half a century, bringing peace and prosperity to his realm. However, at the end of this tranquil period, Geatland had to face a trauma every bit as **intimidating**[16] as Grendel and his mother.

Something You Should Know

　　貝奧武夫眾勇士在雄偉的宮殿大廳 mead-hall 接受隆重款待之後即出發滅敵。mead-hall 在當時文化中象徵艱困世界裡的歡樂地，勇士們暢飲成醉，因未知明日將是何種命運。

Words for Production

7. peril [ˋpɛrəl] *n.* [C][U] 巨大的危險
8. snatch [snætʃ] *v.* 奪走，搶走
9. whirl [hwɝl] *n. sing.* 旋轉；迴旋
10. wrestle [ˋrɛsl̩] *v.* （將…）摔倒
11. clutch [klʌtʃ] *v.* 緊抓，緊握
12. pledge [plɛdʒ] *v.* 發誓；保證
13. courteous [ˋkɝtɪəs] *adj.* 有禮貌的
14. bleak [blik] *adj.* 荒涼的；淒涼的
15. herald [ˋhɛrəld] *v.*
    （尤指透過慶祝或讚揚）宣布
16. intimidating [ɪnˋtɪmə͵detɪŋ] *adj.*
    令人緊張的，嚇人的

Words for Recognition

* deprive [dɪˋpraɪv] *v.* 搶走，剝奪
* ghastly [ˋgæstlɪ] *adj.* 可怕的；令人震驚的

Idioms and Phrases

5. fly into a rage 勃然大怒

Discussion

The heroes in the story are tested for their ability to defeat monsters to safeguard public safety. Do you feel sympathy for the defeated beast Grendel and his mother? Why or why not?

Centuries ago, the last survivor of an ancient race had buried his treasure in a barrow*. A fierce dragon discovered the treasure and jealously guarded it for three hundred years. One day, a thief entered the burial **mound**[17] and stole a cup covered in jewels while the beast slept. The dragon noticed the cup was missing when it awoke. It flew out of the barrow and hunted the intruder, burning everything in its path. The dragon's fury grew when it couldn't find him and it attacked the Geats every night. The dragon found King Beowulf's hall and burned it to the ground.

Though he was now very old, Beowulf felt it was his duty to defend his people against this **hostile**[18] creature. He put on his armor and journeyed to the dragon's barrow with eleven of his bravest warriors. Beowulf challenged the dragon to fight. The dragon attacked Beowulf, who had lost much strength in his old age. Nevertheless, he fought heroically until the dragon bit him into his neck and seriously wounded him.

Thereafter, all but one of Beowulf's companions fled in terror. Wiglaf, the remaining warrior, resolved to be loyal to his king even if it meant death. The brave warrior thrust his sword into the dragon's belly, giving Beowulf the opportunity to take out a knife and stab the creature in its side. The dragon was fatally wounded and died. When Beowulf's neck began to throb* and burn, he realized the dragon's bite was poisonous.

The dying Beowulf asked Wiglaf to take care of his people. Wiglaf was ashamed of the cowardly warriors for not helping to save their leader. Beowulf was given a magnificent funeral by the Geats. His body was laid on a pyre* which was then set alight*. His **remains**[19] were placed in a barrow on a cliff overlooking the sea, so that sailors voyaging by would see the mighty warrior's tomb. The Geats mourned their great leader and were fearful, for their future seemed **gloomy**[20] now that Beowulf could no longer protect them.

Something You Should Know

貝奧武夫壯烈殉國之後，被安排隆重的火葬，這是非基督徒的傳統葬禮，也出現在中古時期亞瑟王 (King Arthur) 的故事裡，亞瑟王死後被置於木舟中，點火之後任其漂流。正統基督徒因為奉行教義中「塵歸塵，土歸土」(Ashes to ashes, dust to dust) 的訓令，人死後要舉行土葬，在地底靜待最後審判日到來。

Words for Production

17. mound [maʊnd] *n.* [C] 土堆；墓塚
18. hostile [ˋhɑstl] *adj.* 不友好的，敵對的
19. remains [rɪˋmenz] *n. pl.* 遺體，遺骸
20. gloomy [ˋglumɪ] *adj.* 沮喪的；無望的

Words for Recognition

* barrow [ˋbæro] *n.* [C] 古墳，古塚
* throb [θrɑb] *v.* 抽痛
* pyre [paɪr] *n.* [C] 火葬堆
* alight [əˋlaɪt] *adj.* 燃燒的；著火的

Idioms and Phrases

6. burn sth to the ground 徹底燒毀 …

Discussion

After you finish reading the story, what do you think of Beowulf as a hero who has finally succumbed to old age and death?

一、閱讀測驗 (Reading Comprehension)

1. Which of the following statements is **NOT** true about Grendel's mother?
    (A) She dwelt in the lake which was filled with monstrous creatures.
    (B) She killed Aeschere before taking Grendel's arm away from the wall.
    (C) Beowulf used his own sword to slice her neck and then killed her.
    (D) At first, Beowulf couldn't overcome her and was losing the battle.

2. Which of the following descriptions is true about the characters?
    (A) King Hygelac was Beowulf's uncle.
    (B) Aeschere was King Hrothgar's only son.
    (C) Breca was one of Beowulf's worst enemies.
    (D) Wiglaf was King Hrothgar's counselor.

3. How did Beowulf die in the end?
    (A) He was seriously ill and died peacefully in his bed.
    (B) He died from a deadly bite in his neck from a dragon.
    (C) He was killed by a wicked warrior in a fierce battle.
    (D) He drank some wine that was poisoned by accident.

4. What is the main purpose of this article?
    (A) To explain why the story of Beowulf is so popular now.
    (B) To demonstrate that Beowulf also had some defects.
    (C) To prove that Beowulf was King Hrothgar's most trusted warrior.
    (D) To briefly introduce the life and heroic deeds of Beowulf.

二、字彙填充 (Fill in the Blanks)

_____ 1. This c_____s young man has made a good impression on the interviewer.

_____ 2. The e_____t candidate finally persuaded most of the voters to elect him as their new mayor.

_____ 3. After being caught cheating on the exam and severely punished, Thomas p_____ed not to do it again.

三、引導式翻譯 (Guided Translation)

1. 當 Kevin 一發現他的車子被偷時，他馬上就勃然大怒。
    As soon as Kevin found that his car had been stolen, he _____ _____ _____ _____ .

2. 一位年輕人毫不猶豫地跳入河中去救那個溺水的小女孩。
    A young man _____ _____ the river without hesitation to rescue that drowning girl.

3. 昨晚有一名縱火犯把這棟舊木屋徹底燒毀了。
    An arsonist _____ this old wooden house _____ _____ _____ last night.

賞析

　　《貝奧武夫》的故事呈現一系列的英雄事蹟，描述現今英國人先祖日耳曼民族 (Germanic peoples) 的勇士如何保家衛國，對抗自然世界的猛獸妖怪。一位真英雄必備兩樣條件：一是門第血統，二是個人威望。這樣的英雄是當時社會的核心棟樑，也是這首詩的核心主題。故事中稱呼英雄人物，例如：貝奧武夫和其他國王，總不忘稱呼他們父親的名號，意謂年輕一代必得不辱家聲傳承英名。日耳曼族英雄不但要體能膽識過人，還要有其他的領袖特質，例如：誠信、自我犧牲、愛民親民等。

　　另外，英雄藉著個人威望塑造他獨有的特質。這個故事頌揚現世的成就，基本上弘揚的是異教徒的文化精髓，不相信有來生或靈魂的不朽存在。因此，英雄的一世英名便是他不朽的印記，英名流傳千古萬世便是對他最大的認可。

　　這首詩以古日耳曼語口傳數百年，到了西元八至十世紀之間以古日耳曼語西撒克遜方言寫成文字，押首韻（同一行詩中幾個字的字首子音相同，例如：**dim, darken, death/winter went wild in the waves**），這是盎格魯—撒克遜時期（又稱古英文時期——Old English）英國文學詩作的特色。它是一首哀悼詩，悼念一位英雄的凋零，雖力拼強敵得勝，但終究不敵大自然的律法，身故留名。

　　故事情節發展包括三個部分，都聚焦英雄和外在敵對力量的抗爭。第一部分描述海中巨怪格倫戴爾肆虐，造成丹麥人 (Danes) 將士的死傷。貝奧武夫從基特（Geatland，現今瑞典南部）前來救援，擊退格倫戴爾。第二部分寫格倫戴爾的母親出現為子復仇，反遭貝奧武夫追趕至深海巢穴消滅。第三部分寫貝奧武夫繼承王位，經過數十年英明統治，在垂老之年突然有巨龍出現傷民，貝奧武夫犧牲自己，屠龍除患。

　　在故事中惡海扮演一個無聲的角色，象徵那個文明未開化的時期，自然界對人類的無情考驗，其中的海怪更是測試英雄真本色的嚴峻力量。這個時期的英雄也必須是善泳者，如貝奧武夫，加上過人的體力和智慧，終能勝出，打敗宰制自然界的邪惡勢力。故事中有一段描寫貝奧武夫年輕時與好友布瑞卡 (Breca) 較量泳技，在翻滾的浪濤間，五晝夜未曾停歇，日夜不斷有海獸欺身，意圖吞噬他，幸有盔甲護身，利劍在手，加以超強的體力與泳技，貝奧武夫終能斬殺海獸，從這場嚴酷的競賽勝出。北歐日耳曼族的故居環繞著深海，酷寒之地，不比南歐蔚藍暖洋。大海是生存的終極考驗，也是淬煉心志的大自然無情的力量。

　　流傳至今的古英文文學（西元十一世紀前）作品寥寥可數，語言也與現代英文相去甚遠。《貝奧武夫》被公認為英國文學的開端，寫的是現今英國的祖輩英雄，呈現那個遙遠時代的價值和感傷。本文只能盡量保存原先繁雜故事的精華，突顯那個時代所景仰的特質和精神，藉以和後來如繁花盛葉的英國文學作品互為參照賞析。

Chapter 2 *Utopia*

關於作者

　　湯瑪斯·摩爾 (Thomas More, 1478–1535) 出生於倫敦，是文藝復興時期英國知名的思想家與政治家。雙親家世尊貴，祖輩多人曾於公會、市政廳和朝廷擔任要職，並於閒暇之餘投資商業，雖非貴族，但家境富裕、家風良好，到父輩時得以進入愛德華四世和亨利七世的樞密院，尤其與莫頓主教（Bishop John Morton，日後升任為大主教 Archbishop）交好，對摩爾的未來成就影響深遠。

　　摩爾由父親安排，幼年即受嚴格教育，熟讀當時的國際語言拉丁文，為他日後進入法律和政治領域奠定紮實的基礎。摩爾在年少時前往莫頓大主教的府邸，成為一名見習童生。莫頓府邸猶如一所學校，摩爾在此受到知識的啟蒙，並接受政經實務訓練，不僅是提前的朝務見習，對於個人修為更有幫助。摩爾也從莫頓身上學習到這位國之重臣的外交與內政能力。莫頓並培養摩爾進入牛津大學就讀，兩年之後轉到倫敦著名的律師學院專修法律。

　　1499 年摩爾結識人文主義者伊拉斯默斯 (Desiderius Erasmus) 和科勒 (John Colet) 等人，結成好友。1505 年與第一任妻子結婚，1511 年元配病逝，摩爾再婚。摩爾終其一生篤信天主教，但同時飽讀希臘羅馬古典著作，優游於聖經教義與希羅經典傳統之間。後得國王亨利八世賞識，提拔為首相，但終因不認同英王的暴虐剛愎，且為了離婚再娶而自立英國國教，摩爾與英王漸行漸遠，在 1535 年因不願隨亨利八世脫離天主教會而被斬首。1935 年天主教會冊封摩爾為聖徒。

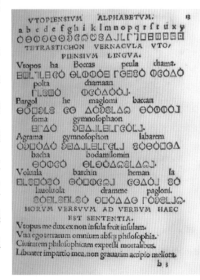

▲ 1516 年第一版《烏托邦》首頁。

湯瑪斯‧摩爾年表

1478

出生於倫敦；父 Sir John More 為知名法官

1492-1493

於牛津接受基礎教育；在坎特伯里大主教莫頓 (John Morton) 府邸擔任見習童生

1494-1498

於倫敦律師學院 (Inns of Court) 學習法律

1499

結識伊拉斯默斯 (Erasmus)、科勒 (John Colet)

1504

贏得選舉，進入國會

1505

第一次婚姻，有四個兒女

1510

擔任倫敦副司法處長

1511

元配病故；第二次婚姻

1516

《烏托邦》於魯汶 (Louvain)（現今比利時）出版

1517

入朝任亨利八世 (Henry VIII) 祕書；出使歐陸；筆伐馬丁‧路德 (Martin Luther)。《烏托邦》於法國巴黎再版

1518

3 月《烏托邦》於瑞士巴塞爾 (Basel) 三版
11 月《烏托邦》於瑞士巴塞爾四版

1523

出任下議院議長

1529-1532

擔任首相

1532-1535

拒絕簽署亨利八世的《至尊法案》(*Acts of Superemacy*)，被囚於倫敦塔，在 1535 年被處死刑

1886

領受天主教會宣福禮 (Beatification)

1935

被天主教會尊為聖徒 (Canonization)

During his journey through Europe, Thomas More encountered many fascinating people, but a chance meeting in Belgium* led to his most compelling discovery of all. More was pleased to meet Peter Giles, a citizen of the city Antwerp. Giles was a very merry, pleasant, and well-learned man, who introduced More to an old man. Raphael Hythloday, a sagacious* and widely traveled man with many life experiences, had a long beard and a weathered, sunburned face.

Hythloday had many opinions about civilization and politics, which he was not shy about sharing. As the three men discussed these ideas, a debate emerged about what **obligation**[1] each person has to play an active role in his community. Both More and Giles believed that a man of experience and **integrity**[2] should be of service to his country and mankind. In particular, More felt that a man of Hythloday's intelligence would be most useful as an advisor to kings and princes. By giving virtuous* opinions to the men in power, who might then choose to heed his advice, Hythloday could do the most good.

Refusing to follow the advice of More and Giles on entering public service, Hythloday criticized the political situations he observed in many European countries. Instead of working for the good of all people, Hythloday felt that kings had tendencies to wage wars in order to conquer new territories and gain more power. Money and other resources were often lost on these fruitless **endeavors**[3], **spiraling**[4] the kings' subjects

into a cycle of poverty and **starvation**[5]. Hythloday also criticized the kings' use of **execution**[6] to punish crimes, as well as the practice of **enclosure**[7], denying people access to common land.

More thought that philosophers such as Hythloday must work amongst people in real situations to effect change, rather than simply produce **lofty**[8] ideals that had no grounding in reality. Political systems were slow to change, so for the sake of expediency*, More also recognized that it was necessary to work within flawed systems to make them better, rather than starting from scratch.

The conversation of More, Giles and Hythloday was interrupted while they enjoyed a pleasant dinner. As they continued their discussion, the topic turned to Hythloday's recent travel to the island of Utopia. After encounters with many different people in lands across the world, Hythloday was eager to share what he learned about Utopia, which has its own unique customs.

Utopia is an island shaped like a crescent*, with two narrow passageways at each end through which the sea flows. The interior part of the island is a peaceful haven*, with gentle waves and sandy shorelines, while the exterior, with lands that face the wider sea, features rough and rocky coasts. The geography makes it difficult for strangers to enter the interior part of the island, unless guided by the Utopians themselves.

Something You Should Know

前四段的敘事方法採用古典修辭學的「對話」(dialogue) 技巧，或稱「辯論」(debate)，利用兩方各陳己見，呈現一個議題的不同角度。這個技巧目的在拓廣思考的層面，不在決定哪一方輸贏。

Words for Production

1. obligation [ˌɑbləˈgeʃən] *n.* [C][U] 義務；責任
2. integrity [ɪnˈtɛgrətɪ] *n.* [U] 正直；誠實
3. endeavor [ɪnˈdɛvɚ] *n.* [C][U] 嘗試
4. spiral [ˈspaɪrəl] *v.* （形勢）急劇惡化；呈螺旋式上升（或下降）
5. starvation [starˈveʃən] *n.* [U] 飢餓
6. execution [ˌɛksɪˈkjuʃən] *n.* [C][U] 死刑；處決
7. enclosure [ɪnˈkloʒɚ] *n.* [C][U] 圈地
8. lofty [ˈlɔftɪ] *adj.* 崇高的；高傲的

Words for Recognition

* Belgium [ˈbɛldʒɪəm] *n.* 比利時
* sagacious [səˈgeʃəs] *adj.* 聰慧的
* virtuous [ˈvɝtʃʊəs] *adj.* 道德高尚的
* expediency [ɪkˈspidɪənsɪ] *n.* 權宜之計
* crescent [ˈkrɛsn̩t] *n.* [C] 新月形（物）
* haven [ˈhevən] *n.* [C] 安全的地方；和平之地

Idioms and Phrases

1. play a role in sth 扮演…角色
2. from scratch 從頭開始

Discussion

Who do you agree with in the debate, More or Hythloday, regarding the topic of entering public service?

The countryside and the cities of Utopia depend on one another to function well, and they enjoy a close relationship. In the country, each farm is run by no fewer than 40 people. Every year, a number of citizens from the city come to live in the country, taking the place of those who have worked at least one year on a farm. In this way, all Utopians are taught critical skills in **cultivating**[9] the land, and no group of people gets stuck doing all of the work. There are 54 cities, none of them further than a journey's distance on foot away from each other. Amaurot is the capital. The city is full of gardens with plentiful fruit, vegetables and herbs growing. The streets are wide and clean, and all of the houses are set in orderly rows. There is nothing in any house that is private or belongs to one person, and in fact, every ten years people change houses.

Every thirty families or a single farm chooses an officer to represent them every year. The society's governing body is responsible for choosing a magistrate*, who is selected by secret election to serve for a lifetime. All of the other offices are held for one year. Any matters that concern the kingdom must be discussed before the council for three days. Holding a discussion outside the council chambers is an offense punishable by death. This decree is intended to prevent the magistrate and the traitors from **conspiring**[10] to oppress the people or change Utopia from a republic into a **tyranny**[11].

Gold and jewelry have a completely different value in Utopia than they do in the rest of the world. While the Utopians highly prize iron, which is essential in forging* the tools necessary for survival, they do not treasure gold. Rather, gold is used to create household items like chamber pots. Pearls are gathered by the seaside and given to children to play with as if they were rocks. Precious jewels are considered commonplace items, not to be valued for more than what they are—simply elements of the earth.

Something You Should Know

在烏托邦的故事當中，你會發現有兩種時態：過去式和現在式。使用兩種不同時態的原因是因為三人會面有具體的時空背景，因此用過去式。舉例來說：The conversation of More, Giles and Hythloday was interrupted while they enjoyed a pleasant dinner.。而描述烏托邦的體制，可以視為對某件親身體驗的事實的陳述，因此用現在式。舉例來說：Utopia is an island shaped like a crescent, with two narrow passageways at each end through which the sea flows.。

Utopians all learn the skills of agriculture, but beyond farming their occupations include masonry*, carpentry* and cloth-making. While every man and woman masters a craft with diligence, the time Utopians spend working is strictly limited to only six hours a day. The rest is devoted to rest, meals and leisure time. Many Utopians attend lectures on all sorts of topics, such as playing music, or tending their gardens, simply for the pleasure and intellectual **stimulation**[12].

All men and women are educated from childhood onwards in music, logic, **arithmetic**[13] and geometry. They have also continued to study astronomy, observing the patterns of the moon, stars and sun. However, the study of virtue and pleasure is one of their chief pursuits. Utopians are very interested in exploring the idea of happiness, constantly asking the question: what constitutes a happy life? They believe that the point of humanity is to bring health and comfort to each individual and especially to minimize the pain and suffering of others. To keep others from pleasure, while seeking one's own, is simply wrong.

Words for Production

9. cultivate [ˋkʌltəˌvet] *v.* 耕作；栽培
10. conspire [kənˋspaɪr] *v.* 共謀；密謀
11. tyranny [ˋtɪrənɪ] *n.* [U] 專制統治，暴政
12. stimulation [ˌstɪmjəˋleʃən] *n.* [U] 刺激；興奮作用
13. arithmetic [ˌærɪθˋmɛtɪk] *n.* [U] 算數

Words for Recognition

* magistrate [ˋmædʒɪsˌtret] *n.* [C] 地方法官
* forge [fɔrdʒ] *v.* 鍛造；製作
* masonry [ˋmesn̩rɪ] *n.* [U] 石工；石建築
* carpentry [ˋkɑrpəntrɪ] *n.* [U] 木工；木工製品

Idioms and Phrases

3. no fewer than 不少於，多達

Discussion

A number of values commonly accepted by most people of our world are reversed in Utopia, for example, the values we give to gold and jewelry. Can you see this reversal happening in our society? Give your reasons.

Utopians do not view slavery as a social system, but turn a prisoner taken from battle or any Utopian who has committed a terrible crime into a slave. Slaves do menial work, such as butchering, for the entire state.

Marriage is reserved for those older than eighteen. Sex before marriage is strictly forbidden and severely punished, for the Utopians believe that if everyone gave in to this vice, very few would choose marriage. They do, however, have the custom of allowing potential grooms and brides to see each other without clothes on before agreeing to marry. They believe that a long-lasting marriage is more likely if both parties know exactly what they are getting. Most marriages are not broken until death, except in cases of **adultery**[14] or the rare occurrence of both parties wanting a divorce. The council will only grant a divorce after diligently hearing the matter from both parties, for the Utopians judge it an act of cruelty to cast off a **spouse**[15] unkindly.

Utopians detest* war and will go to great lengths to avoid it. However, both men and women in Utopia have served in the same military that practices daily in case it is ever needed. The only circumstances under which they would consider warfare is in defense of their country, to defeat an invading enemy for diplomatic allies or to deliver a people from the bondage of tyranny. In all other cases, they consider war to be a vainglorious* and abominable* thing.

As for religion, the majority of Utopians believe in one god. This guiding force, the creator of the universe, is viewed as the ruler of the entire world. However, other Utopians worship the sun, the stars, the moon and any number of other religious symbols. One of the oldest laws of their commonwealth is that all are free to believe in whatever they choose. If one would like to lead others to follow their religion, they must do it peacefully and respectfully, with absolutely no violence.

After hearing Hythloday's account of Utopia and its unique customs, More was not wholly **converted**[16] to the Utopian system. Without any use of money, the true **ornament**[17] and honor of a commonwealth could not exist, according to More. However, he regarded some of Utopia's features as good and wished that they could be adopted in Europe.

Something You Should Know

文學作品中常用具體的物來表達抽象的意念，經過一段的時間形成了被廣泛接受的象徵詮釋，例如：紅玫瑰代表熾熱的愛情。摩爾創造的烏托邦是個新月形，它的兩個犄角相距約11哩，形成一座港灣，內港風平浪靜，船隻在內部港口之間來往便利。由於出口狹小，便於防守，敵人入侵不易。入口航道一邊是淺灘，一邊是岩岸，中間遍布礁石，因此外人進入烏托邦一定要有本地領航人帶路，否則性命難保。這樣的造型傳達的意念是：烏托邦是個自給自足、法制典章完備的城邦國。它是個封閉的文化及社會體系，排斥外來的異類因素，國民謹守公民義務，服從法治。烏托邦不是一個開放逍遙歡樂的樂園想像。

▲ 木刻烏托邦島嶼外觀。左下為拉斐爾‧希斯拉德 (Raphael Hythloday) 描述烏托邦島嶼。

Words for Production

14. adultery [ə`dʌltərɪ] *n.* [U] 通姦
15. spouse [spaʊz] *n.* [C] 配偶
16. convert [kən`vɝt] *v.*
    改變信仰（或態度）；歸附
17. ornament [`ɔrnəmənt] *n.* [U]
    裝飾，擺設；點綴

Words for Recognition

* detest [dɪ`tɛst] *v.* 憎恨；厭惡
* vainglorious [ven`glorɪəs] *adj.* 自負的；
    自命不凡的
* abominable [ə`bɑmənəbl̩] *adj.* 可惡的；
    討厭的

Idioms and Phrases

4. cast sth off/cast off sth 拋棄…
5. go to great lengths 竭盡全力

Discussion

Do you think Utopia is an earthly paradise? Why or why not?

一、閱讀測驗 (Reading Comprehension)

1. What's the purpose of this article?

    (A) To introduce an imaginary and unique society.

    (B) To elaborate how to reach an isolated island.

    (C) To demonstrate the author's great intelligence.

    (D) To criticize the corruption of European kings.

2. What can we learn about Hythloday from this article?

    (A) He heard of Utopia from a close friend.

    (B) He was hesitant to share his opinions.

    (C) He was reluctant to enter public service.

    (D) He seldom traveled to foreign countries.

3. Which of the following statements regarding Utopia is **NOT** true?

    (A) Citizens are not allowed to get married until they turn eighteen.

    (B) The huge walls surrounding it prevent strangers from entering it.

    (C) There are fifty-four cities in total and Amaurot is the capital.

    (D) Utopians have the freedom to believe in whatever they choose.

4. In what order did Hythloday describe Utopia?

    (A) Geography → religion → politics → marriage → occupations → education

    (B) Geography → education → politics → religion → occupations → marriage

    (C) Geography → politics → marriage → occupations → religion → education

    (D) Geography → politics → occupations → education → marriage → religion

二、字彙填充 (Fill in the Blanks)

_____ 1. Alice thinks it is her o_____n to take good care of her aged parents.

_____ 2. The people in that country revolted against the t_____y and overthrew it.

_____ 3. Tina's father is a man of i_____y who never tricks others or tells lies.

三、引導式翻譯 (Guided Translation)

1. Wendy 總是竭盡全力去完成每一項任務。

    Wendy always _____ _____ _____ _____ to accomplish every task.

2. 有多達三千人參加了這次的遊行。

    There were _____ _____ _____ 3,000 people taking part in this parade.

3. 既然我們的提案已經被客戶拒絕了，我們就必須再從頭開始。

    Since our proposal has been rejected by our client, we have to start again _____ _____ .

賞析

　　摩爾在 1515 年出使荷蘭安特衛普城，與伊拉斯默斯 (Erasmus) 的好友，時任安特衛普城書記官的彼得・蓋爾斯 (Peter Giles) 見了面。在這趟旅途中摩爾醞釀了《烏托邦》的核心構想，在秋天回到英國時，該書第二部 (Book Two) 描繪烏托邦的草稿已經完成，後來再添加了第一部 (Book One)，藉由主角三人的對話，談論「有才能的人是否應該從政」，最終於 1516 年定稿並出版。《烏托邦》原書以拉丁文撰寫，著眼於歐洲大陸的菁英讀者。此書是摩爾最為人知的傳世之作，後世讀者透過這本像是稜鏡般多面的虛構故事，不斷探索摩爾對烏托邦體制的態度，以及烏托邦理想國的利弊。

　　《烏托邦》出版後，立即轟動知識界，短時間之內即多次再版。此書以對話和引述的敘事模式記錄「摩爾」（學者稱為摩爾在書中的代言人）和一位老水手希斯拉德在安特衛普的偶遇與交談內容。第一部中的談話聚焦當時歐洲和英國政治與社會的腐敗，貧富懸殊、政策失當（圈地運動使得窮人無公地可耕，遂湧入都市偷劫搶騙）以及官員貪腐無度。第二部則描繪理想城邦「烏托邦」，包括它防守嚴密的地理形狀，到尊卑有序、公平正義的社會與經濟制度，以及國民守法、修身利他的法治與倫理教育。烏托邦最受摩爾讚許的特色是它共工共享的公社體制 (commune)，全國沒有富人，但也沒有因飢餓而起盜心的窮人。

　　烏托邦以「法治」為立國安邦的基石，政治體制嚴格施行共和議會制，重要的國事議題都必須在議會中公開討論，首長不得在議場之外聚眾議論，以免遭人懷疑有造反的意圖，如有違反，最重可以處死。烏托邦國民不分男女，都要遵從法律規定，例如：人人第一個職業都是農夫，輪流定期下鄉務農；第二個職業可以自由選擇，例如造路、補鍋等。法律也規定人人每天工作六小時，其餘時間用於運動和聽演講，鍛鍊身體和增長知識。每天早晨進餐之前必須參加晨課，加強對法律的認識，並且於一生中落實法律所規定的一切。烏托邦強調法治教育的重要，目的在確實培育守法的公民。烏托邦不是一個人間樂園 (earthly paradise)，沒有法律約束只有隨性享樂，沒有勞動只有安逸。烏托邦恰恰相反，法治是教育手段，也是目的。

　　摩爾的烏托邦受到柏拉圖《理想國》(*The Republic*) 的啟發，他也啟迪了後世許多仿效公社體制的生活模式，由成員共有共享生產所得。知名的例子有十九世紀 30 年代在美國盛行的傅立葉主義 (Fourierism) 和隨後於波士頓郊外推行的公社組織 (Brook Farm)。古代中國亦有「大同世界」的理念，目的也在闡述一個理性、利他、不虞匱乏的理想社會。然而，也有一些質疑烏托邦理念的人，只追求從眾行為 (conformity)，不認同個體差異，這樣的體制成為無上的威權，最終宰制消弭了個體的自主權。此質疑逐漸衍生出「反烏托邦」(anti-utopia, dystopia) 的思維，奧威爾 (George Orwell) 的小說《動物農莊》(*Animal Farm*) 和赫胥黎 (Aldous Huxley) 的《美麗新世界》(*Brave New World*) 都是大家熟知的反烏托邦文學。或許，要實現一個理想完美的社會是很難達成的，而摩爾對此早就清楚明白。所造之字 utopia，字首的 u 可以同時解讀為 eu（美好）和 ou（沒有）兩義，utopia 一字遂為 eutopia（美好城邦）和 outopia（烏有之邦）的矛盾合體。於是，《烏托邦》一書承載的終究是一則思辯的選擇題，而不是一個實踐的是非題。

Chapter 3 *Doctor Faustus*

關於作者

　　克里斯多福·馬羅（Christopher Marlowe, 1564–1593），英國伊莉莎白時期的劇作家、翻譯家及詩人，與莎士比亞（William Shakespeare）同年出生。馬羅以寫作悲劇及無韻詩（blank verse）聞名。父親是倫敦東南方坎特伯里市的鞋匠。於坎特伯里國王學校（The King's School, Canterbury）中學校就讀，並在 16 歲時進入劍橋大學基督聖體學院（Corpus Christi College）就讀，獲頒的獎學金原意在於培養神職人員。馬羅連續拿了六年獎學金，但是沒有成為神職人員，卻轉而寫起劇本。

　　馬羅短暫的一生波折不斷、撲朔迷離。1587 年他申請就讀母校文學碩士班，劍橋大學本打算拒收他，一種說法是他準備前往法國加入流亡在天主教重鎮荷姆市（Rheims，為現今法國的漢斯 Reims）的英國天主教徒，但是樞密院介入為他洗白，讚揚他為女王進行祕密任務有功，要求大學盡快讓他完成學業頒予學位。馬羅作為女王的密探，偵察避難海外的英國天主教徒，雖然可信，但卻無文字記錄可以佐證。

　　馬羅得到碩士學位之後定居倫敦，時年 23 歲。在短暫但輝煌的六年文學生涯中首先寫了《帖木兒大帝》（*Tamburlaine the Great*）並在倫敦劇院演出，一舉成名。1589 年他出版劇作《浮士德》（*Doctor Faustus*）和《馬爾他的猶太人》（*The Jew of Malta*），1592 年出版劇作《愛德華二世》（*Edward II*），1593 年出版劇作《巴黎大屠殺》（*The Massacre at Paris*），其他作品包括翻譯拉丁文經典以及詩作。馬羅性格暴烈，思想行為狂悖不羈，經常在街頭與人衝突鬧事，並曾因此被捕下獄，後來更遭人檢舉發表無神論並有褻瀆上帝的言行。1593 年春天他在倫敦東南郊德普特福德（Deptford）一個酒館與一幫損友為酒帳起衝突，鬥毆時遭匕首刺傷身亡，結束二十九年的人生。

克里斯多福・馬羅年表

1564

出生於坎特伯里；父 John Marlowe 為鞋匠，母 Catherine Arthur 為教士之女

1580

於劍橋大學基督聖體學院就讀，並領取未來要任神職人員的學生獎學金

1584

畢業於劍橋大學基督聖體學院，逐漸成為極富盛名的作家

1584-1586

擔任新朝廷的密探，前往法國荷姆市

1587-1592

完成《浮士德》(*Doctor Faustus*)

1587-1593

移居倫敦

1593

英國政府下令通緝馬婁，但沒有列出任何罪狀。同年五月於德普特福德的一個酒館與人爭執，被匕首刺死

◀ 此插圖為木版畫，出現於《浮士德》後期版本的書中。

法國浪漫主義畫家歐仁・德拉克羅瓦 (Eugène Delacroix) 的平版印刷作品「Mephistopheles in the sky」，描繪惡天使——梅菲斯托費勒斯 (Mephistopheles)。 ▶

Doctor Faustus was born into a poor family in Germany. He was a gifted student and gained a place at the prestigious university of Wittenberg. He specialized in theology*, earning the degree of Doctor of Divinity*. Faustus then became an expert in many other fields, and was a **renowned**[1] scholar.

Yet, despite acquring all his knowledge, Faustus was not **content**[2]. He had mastered logic, medicine, law and theology. Nevertheless, he was still subject to the limitations of every mortal man. Faustus had **contempt**[3] for Christians who believed human beings were sinners* who could only be saved by having faith in God. He felt morally superior to ordinary men. Faustus wanted more power and pleasure unavailable to his fellow men. The famous scholar therefore considered turning to black magic to satisfy his desires. He decided to invite his friends Valdes and Cornelius, who practiced the dark magic, to dine with him.

While waiting, he was visited by a good angel and an evil angel. The former pleaded with Faustus to avoid black magic, otherwise he risked being damned eternally. The latter encouraged Faustus to explore this art to have god-like powers. Faustus was unable to resist the evil angel's **temptations**[4] and fondly imagined that he would have all his desires satisfied in the future.

When his friends arrived, they practiced some secret incantations* so that Faustus could **summon**[5] spirits to obey his commands. When they left, he decided to employ his newly acquired knowledge. Faustus began his incantations. The devil Mephistophilis suddenly appeared. This gave Faustus confidence in his magic powers, and he demanded that the devil obey his commands. However, Mephistophilis stated that he would need his master Lucifer's permission first.

He told Faustus that Lucifer had been God's favorite angel but he had launched a **rebellion**[6] against him. As a result, he and his followers were damned eternally in hell. Faustus argued that Mephistophilis could not be in hell if he was there in his study. Mephistophilis replied that "this is hell, nor am I out of it," for hell was the state of being banned from heaven. The devil even warned Faustus not to endanger his soul by seeking powers from Lucifer.

However, Faustus refused to believe that hell was so terrible, and asked Mephistophilis to offer Lucifer a deal. Faustus pledged to deliver his soul to Lucifer if he could have Mephistophilis as his servant for twenty-four years. Mephistophilis promised to return at midnight with Lucifer's answer.

The good angel and evil angel appeared again. Faustus rejected the good angel's advice to "think of heaven" and was persuaded by the evil angel to "think of honor and of wealth." Mephistophilis then returned. He informed Faustus that Lucifer had agreed to the deal. The price would be Faustus' soul. In addition, Faustus would need to sign the contract in his own blood.

Faustus willingly cut his arm, and started to sign. However, his blood suddenly stopped flowing as if reacting against the unholy deed. Mephistophilis went to **fetch**[7] some fire to thin Faustus' blood. Despite this **implicit**[8] warning, Faustus insisted on continuing. When Mephistophilis brought the bowl of fire, Faustus finished signing. He was then shocked to see the words *homo, fuge*—Latin for "run away, man"—on his arm. Faustus recklessly ignored this **explicit**[9] warning and submitted the contract to Mephistophilis, convincing himself that "hell's a fable."

Words for Production

1. renowned [rɪ`naʊnd] *adj.* 著名的
2. content [kən`tɛnt] *adj.* 滿意的;滿足的;知足的
3. contempt [kən`tɛmpt] *n.* [U] 蔑視
4. temptation [tɛmp`teʃən] *n.* [C][U] 引誘;誘惑
5. summon [`sʌmən] *v.* 傳喚;召集
6. rebellion [rɪ`bɛljən] *n.* [C][U] 反叛
7. fetch [fɛtʃ] *v.* (去)拿來,取回
8. implicit [ɪm`plɪsɪt] *adj.* 不明言的
9. explicit [ɪk`splɪsɪt] *adj.* 清楚明白的

Words for Recognition

* theology [θi`ɑlədʒɪ] *n.* [U] 神學,宗教信仰學
* Divinity [dɪ`vɪnətɪ] *n.* [U] 神學
* sinner [`sɪnɚ] *n.* [C] 罪人
* incantation [ˌɪnkæn`teʃən] *n.* [C][U] 咒語;念咒

Idioms and Phrases

1. specialize in sth 專門研究,專攻…
2. be subject to sth 遭受,承受…

Discussion

What are the positive qualities, if any, you find in Faustus, a damned soul in the Christian sense?

Something You Should Know

黑巫術(black magic或稱dark magic)指魔鬼所施,為了自身利益與上帝作對的超自然能力。聖經中描述很多上帝所施的奇蹟,例如:創造宇宙萬物以及耶穌復活等。撒旦和他的黨羽也具有超能力,但是目的是為了毀滅上帝所完成的善果。屬於撒旦的超能力稱為「黑巫術」,因其邪惡並與光明的上帝對抗。

Consequently, Faustus indulged in the various pleasures he was able to experience by commanding Mephistophilis. He also requested him to satisfy his curiosity about the universe. However, when he asked who created the world, Mephistophilis would not answer. He said he could only respond to questions that were not against the kingdom of hell, and that Faustus should concern himself solely with damnation. Faustus was alarmed and **pondered**[10] whether he still had the opportunity to return to God.

The good and evil angels reappeared, the evil one telling him, "Too late," and the good one, "Never too late, if Faustus will repent*." Faustus panicked and called to Christ, "Help save distressed Faustus' soul!" Lucifer himself now appeared. Faustus was intimidated by his menacing expression. Lucifer warned Faustus that by mentioning Christ he was breaking his contract. When Faustus subsequently vowed "never to look to heaven," Lucifer promised him great rewards.

To convince Faustus of the benefits of his contract, Lucifer summoned the Seven Deadly Sins to parade before him, to reveal the delights of sins. They came in one by one and spoke to Faustus. Faustus said the show delighted his soul and renewed his **commitment**[11] before Lucifer departed.

Faustus now took full advantage of his magic powers. He discovered the secrets of astronomy by viewing the clouds, planets and stars from the top of Mount Olympus. He travelled in a **chariot**[12] drawn by dragons around the world, and then decided to tour the great kingdoms of the earth accompanied by Mephistophilis.

Their first destination was the Pope's court in Rome. There they disguised themselves as two cardinals* and visited the Pope. The Pope told them to arrange the execution of Bruno, whom the German emperor had attempted to make the Pope. However, Faustus and Mephistophilis helped him escape to Germany. Later, at a feast the real cardinals were **humiliated**[13] because they had no knowledge of the Pope's orders. They were accused of **treason**[14] and sentenced to death.

Faustus commanded Mephistophilis to make him invisible*. He then insulted the Pope and snatched his food and drink. The guests believed a ghost was haunting them, and the Pope called priests to cast out the ghost. Faustus was angry when the Pope made the sign of the cross. When the priests arrived and began their curses, Faustus and Mephistophilis threw fireworks into the chamber and fled.

Faustus and Mephistophilis now visited the emperor of Germany's court. The monarch thanked and praised Faustus for freeing Bruno. Flattered, Faustus offered his services to the emperor who asked Faustus to show him Alexander the Great and his lover. Faustus cast a spell and the ancient Greek emperor appeared. The court watched Alexander kill the Persian king Darius III of Persia and put the dead king's crown on his lover's head. The spirits then saluted the German emperor before vanishing.

Something You Should Know

善天使與惡天使是中古時期英國文學和街頭劇場常用的表現技巧,代表善惡之間的對立,普遍以寓言體的抽象形式,由兩個角色直言較勁,企圖影響徬徨不定的主角。善天使為上帝的僕役,無私的效忠上帝;而惡天使則是撒旦的奴僕,與上帝交戰。

Words for Production

10. ponder [ˋpɑndɚ] *v.* 沉思,考慮
11. commitment [kəˋmɪtmənt] *n.* [C][U] 忠誠;承諾
12. chariot [ˋtʃærɪət] *n.* [C] 雙輪馬車
13. humiliate [hjuˋmɪlɪˏet] *v.* 羞辱
14. treason [ˋtrizṇ] *n.* [U] 叛國(罪)

Words for Recognition

* repent [rɪˋpɛnt] *v.* 後悔;懺悔
* cardinal [ˋkɑrdnəl] *n.* [C] 樞機主教,紅衣主教
* invisible [ɪnˋvɪzəbl] *adj.* 看不見的

Idioms and Phrases

3. cast a spell 施魔法,念咒語

Discussion

Hell, as described in *the Bible*, is a place of burning fire and everlasting pain. Do you find a similar description of hell in other religions?

Faustus also amused himself by playing spiteful* tricks on people. One day he met a horse dealer and sold his horse cheaply to him. He told his victim not to ride the horse into water. Nevertheless, the dealer ignored Faustus' warning and the horse turned into a bundle of straw. He was angry and attacked Faustus while he was sleeping. Faustus' leg came off when the dealer pulled it and ran off with it. Later, he was shocked to see that Faustus still had two legs and realized that he had been tricked again.

Hearing of Faustus' wicked deeds, a holy old man came to try to save his soul. He warned him to "leave this damned art" or else it would be too late for God's forgiveness. He said there was an angel over Faustus' head who could still pour mercy into his soul. Faustus was shaken and regretted his foolish bargain with Lucifer. Mephistophilis quickly **intervened**[15] and accused Faustus of being a **traitor**[16]. He threatened to tear him to pieces if he turned to God. Faustus was intimidated and confirmed his vow to Lucifer.

As the end of the contract drew near, Faustus **bade**[17] Mephistophilis bring the legendary Helen of Troy to be his lover. When she appeared, Faustus was overwhelmed by her beauty and **exclaimed**[18], "Was this the face that launched a thousand ships?" Faustus asked her to "make me immortal with a kiss." He then kissed her, hoping he could live with her eternally.

Yet, it could not be. Faustus' twenty-four year contract had **expired**[19]. On the final eve, Faustus was visited by three scholars. They were astonished by how pale and ill he looked. Faustus informed them of his **pact**[20] with Lucifer and that he would soon "be in hell forever." The scholars urged him to pray for **salvation**[21], but Faustus realized his pleas would be of no use.

The good angel and evil angel visited Faustus for the last time. The good angel **lamented**[22] that Faustus was doomed to eternal damnation, while the bad angel showed Faustus a vision of the horror of hell. Then, the clock struck eleven. Faustus desperately prayed for time to slow down and for Christ to save him.

When midnight came, there was a terrible thunderstorm and the devils came to carry Faustus away. The scholars returned the following day. They had heard terrible **shrieks**[23] and cries for help during the tempest. They found Faustus' body torn apart. Out of respect for Faustus as a fellow scholar, they decided to gather his limbs and bury them at a **solemn**[24] funeral.

Something You Should Know

地獄常稱冥府，指人死後所到之處。此概念並非基督教特有，東西方文化都有對死後世界的想像。中國釋道文化勸人為善，因此強調做惡之人死後會下十八層地獄，受刀山油鍋之苦。西方基督教教義則以信仰基督為首條戒律，以上帝為唯一真神，信祂得永生，反之若違反教義則墜入魔道，必下地獄不得超生。基督教的地獄永遠燃燒著硫磺火，沒有亮光，只有永恆的昏暝，墜入地獄的靈魂永遠承受硫磺火的燒灼，感受無盡的痛苦。

Words for Production

15. intervene [ˌɪntɚˋvin] *v.* 干涉，干預
16. traitor [ˋtretɚ] *n.* [C] 背叛者，叛徒
17. bid [bɪd] *v.* 請求；打招呼，致意
18. exclaim [ɪkˋsklem] *v.* 呼喊，驚叫
19. expire [ɪkˋspaɪr] *v.* 到期，期滿
20. pact [pækt] *n.* [C] 契約；條約
21. salvation [sælˋveʃən] *n.* [U] 救贖
22. lament [ləˋmɛnt] *v.* 對…感到悲痛
23. shriek [ʃrik] *n.* [C] 尖叫
24. solemn [ˋsɑləm] *adj.* 莊嚴的，嚴肅的

Words for Recognition

* spiteful [ˋspaɪtfəl] *adj.*
  惡意的；故意使人苦惱的

Idioms and Phrases

4. run off with sth 偷了…逃走
5. pour sth into sth 向…投入大量…
6. turn to sb/sth 求助於…

Discussion

Do you think Faustus deserves his tragic downfall? Why?

一、閱讀測驗 (Reading Comprehension)

1. Why did Faustus turn to black magic in the first place?

    (A) He was a religious Christian and wanted to study and destroy it.

    (B) He needed to learn how to use the magic powers to revive his dead parents.

    (C) He was very greedy and regarded himself as morally superior to others.

    (D) He was haunted by evil spirits and wanted to use it to drive them away.

2. What happened when Faustus' contract with Lucifer was going to expire?

    (A) Faustus fell in love with Helen of Troy and longed to stay with her for good.

    (B) Faustus summoned Alexander the Great to stage a show to entertain himself.

    (C) Faustus amused himself by playing a malicious trick on a horse dealer.

    (D) Lucifer appeared in front of Faustus and agreed to renew the contract.

3. According to this story, which of the following is **NOT** true?

    (A) The good angel and evil angel visited Faustus four times in total.

    (B) Faustus was satisfied with the contract and never regretted signing it.

    (C) A number of scholars held a solemn funeral for Faustus after his death.

    (D) Mephistophilis said that hell was the state of being banned from heaven.

4. What lesson can we learn from this story?

    (A) The pursuit of knowledge and fame can sometimes lead us to engage in terrible deeds.

    (B) When we make a deal with others, we are supposed to abide by it whatever happens.

    (C) When we do something immoral, praying to God is the only way to attain salvation.

    (D) We should not be selfish and should make good use of our powers to benefit others.

二、字彙填充 (Fill in the Blanks)

_____ 1. The U.S. is determined to i_____e in the country's civil war to prevent more people from dying.

_____ 2. The man was accused of t_____n because he had betrayed his country.

_____ 3. Robert is a r_____d professor who is often invited to deliver speeches.

三、引導式翻譯 (Guided Translation)

1. 那個巫婆念了咒語，當場把英俊的王子變成一隻醜陋的青蛙。

    The witch _____ _____ _____ and turned the handsome prince into an ugly frog on the spot.

2. Stephanie 是一名專精於當代藝術的知名學者。

    Stephanie is a distinguished scholar who _____ _____ contemporary art.

3. 昨晚一名盜賊闖入 Paul 的房子，並偷了大量現金逃走了。

    A burglar broke into Paul's house last night and _____ _____ _____ much cash.

賞析

　　浮士德的傳奇起源於中古時期歐陸國家，後來逐漸成為世界諸國流傳甚廣的故事。故事原型可能來自新約聖經《使徒行傳》中有關西門‧馬吉斯 (Simon Magus) 行使巫術的傳說。這種聖經中多所描述的巫術，對信徒具有警惕的教化功用，訓令他們遠離黑巫術，否則將墜入萬劫不復的地獄，靈魂永遠得不到救贖。

　　十五世紀中葉的德國流傳一則故事，關於某人把靈魂出賣給魔鬼，用來交換凡人無法施行的魔法。這個故事版本甚多，其中姓氏為浮士德的主角名字有海因里希 (Heinrich)、約翰 (Johan) 和喬治 (George) 等不一而足。這些不同名字的浮士德共同的特點都是巫術師，故事圍繞著這名主角，經過穿鑿附會，造就浮士德成為對基督徒的終極警示。

　　馬羅的《浮士德》沿襲中古時期的版本，故事情節分為三段，首段寫德國威騰堡 (Wittenberg) 的知名學者浮士德急欲探索宇宙的祕密：人從哪裡來？造物主是誰？他的才智過人，人類知識的極限（諸如神學、法律、醫學等）已經無法滿足他的求知慾望。他遂與魔鬼簽約，以自己的靈魂交換魔鬼給予的二十四年的超自然能力。中段寫他有了超能力之後上天入地，也到了羅馬教廷大鬧取樂。末段寫他最後的結局，於哀嚎聲中被魔鬼拖入地獄。

　　在原作的一開始，浮士德的臺詞中有許多豪氣干雲的段落，代表了文藝復興時代，歐洲人想掙脫傳統基督教謙卑畏神的教條，例如：浮士德想要縱橫跨越全世界，前往印度探礦取金，潛入大洋探底取珠，建造一道長城圍繞德國全境，並令萊茵河改道環抱威騰堡等。字裡行間洋溢著人本意識的甦醒和萌發，不再甘於充當上帝馴服的綿羊，只能引頸翹盼來世的救贖，而要奮起發揮人的潛能，求取今世的自我成就。

　　《浮士德》劇中神本主義和人本覺醒兩股思潮互相傾軋，但結局依然未能擺脫傳統的命定：浮士德遭到上帝的懲罰，絕望地入了地獄。一個人本中心的浮士德到了十八世紀末的德國，方才現身於歌德的《浮士德》。這位浮士德成功地超越凡人的限制，追求人性的關愛與幸福，雖與魔鬼有約，但最終卻因利人的善念得到救贖，由天使接引上天堂。馬羅的浮士德卻因貪圖滿足私欲，而遭致悲劇下場。這兩則結局迥異的浮士德故事，兩位主角在品德與實際作為上具有天壤之別，一位利己，一位利他，提供最佳的反差，讓讀者深思判斷。兩個浮士德故事的不同結局在於昭示品德的核心價值：「培養知善、樂善與行善的品德素養。」

Chapter 4 *Hamlet*

關於作者

　　威廉·莎士比亞 (William Shakespeare, 1564–1616) 猶如當年文壇的一顆彗星，每當他的劇本演出時，倫敦全城公卿貴族、學者文士和販夫走卒都搶著先睹為快。但是，他的生平卻如一個謎團，遺留下來的確實資料寥寥可數，僅有教堂記錄的諸如生卒年及結婚等重大事件。1564 年，他出生於亞芬河畔的史特拉福 (Stratford-upon-Avon) 小鎮。祖父為佃農，父親開店販售手套和小皮件，有一段時間擔任小鎮鎮長，家境小康。他幼年受過正規的小學教育，略識拉丁文和希臘文。在 18 歲時與安·海瑟薇 (Anne Hathaway) 結婚，生有二女一男。後來倫敦迅速發展為英國經濟與文化中心之際，莎士比亞便離家前往倫敦發展。但是他終於在劇場發跡，成為炙手可熱的劇作家與演員之前的事蹟，卻無可考據，他的名字只有偶爾被當時嫉妒他的文人提起，調侃他是個白丁（沒有受過大學教育），卻在倫敦引領風騷。此次事件發生在 1592 年，有文字記錄，當時莎士比亞 28 歲。

　　莎士比亞一生寫作三十七個劇本（包括悲劇、喜劇和歷史劇），另有十四行詩和其他詩作。1611 年他退休回到故鄉，1616 年過世。當時知名的學者文人強生 (Ben Jonson) 為他寫了一首悼念詩，尊稱他為「亞芬河上的綺美天鵝」("Sweet swan of Avon")，並誇他翱翔在泰晤士河上，絢爛的光彩令伊莉莎白女王和詹姆士國王也目不暇給。莎士比亞的魅力直到今天依然永恆不朽。

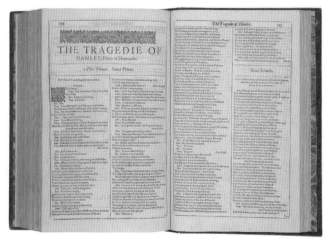

▲ 《哈姆雷特》一劇的首頁，刊於《第一對開本》。

莎士比亞年表

1564

出生於亞芬河畔史特拉福；父 John Shakespeare 做過許多工作，包括農夫、手套商人和市參議員。於亞芬河畔史特拉福的國王學校接受教育。（雖無史料依據，但是大部分的傳記作者認同。）

1582

與安・海瑟薇 (Anne Hathaway) 結婚，兩人共生育了三個孩子

1585-1592

學者將這段期間稱為行蹤成謎的歲月。

1592

出現在倫敦的劇團中

1603

《哈姆雷特》(*Hamlet*) 刊於《第一四開本》

1604

《哈姆雷特》(*Hamlet*) 刊於《第二四開本》

1613

退休回到亞芬河畔史特拉福

1616

逝世

1623

《哈姆雷特》(*Hamlet*) 刊於《第一對開本》

亞芬河畔史特拉福，莎士比亞父親的住宅，▶
歷代認為是莎士比亞的出生地。

◀ 依據考古實證及文獻資料，推測而得的環球劇場樣貌，為一座三層開放式的木製結構。舞臺下方為站票區，觀眾只花一個便士便可觀賞演出。

While studying in Wittenberg in Germany, Prince Hamlet received news that his father, the King of Denmark, had died. Consequently, he returned to the Danish palace at Elsinore castle for the funeral. Hamlet had been the **heir**[1] to the throne. However, his mother, Queen Gertrude, quickly became engaged to his uncle, Claudius. They married two months later, so Claudius became king. The prince stayed in Denmark for the wedding and coronation*. He was bitter that his mother had remarried so soon. Moreover, he **resented**[2] Claudius, regarding him as a man vastly inferior to his father.

At court, Hamlet's loyal friend Horatio informed him about a ghost that he and some castle guards had seen. He said that it looked like Hamlet's father. Hamlet joined them in investigating the ghost around the castle walls that night. When the ghost appeared, the prince rushed to meet it. The ghost **disclosed**[3] that he was Hamlet's father's spirit and that he had been murdered by Claudius. Everyone had believed that he had been bitten by a snake while sleeping in his orchard. In fact, his brother had crept up on him and poured deadly poison in his ears. The ghost commanded Hamlet to "revenge his **foul**[4] and most unnatural murder." Hamlet swore he would kill his uncle for his crime, promising to "sweep to my revenge." Nevertheless, Hamlet feared "the time is out of joint" for decisive action. **Paralyzed**[5] by grief and also upset by his mother's conduct, the prince cursed the fact that he "was born to set it right."

Instead of acting immediately, the troubled prince decided to pretend to be mad. He hoped to fool the king, so he would not regard him as a threat. However, Claudius was **suspicious**[6] because of Hamlet's hostility to him at the wedding. The king asked his councilor, Lord Polonius, to observe Hamlet closely. Polonius had **disapproved**[7] of Hamlet's attraction to his daughter, Ophelia, and had warned her not to encourage him. When Ophelia told him that Hamlet had just seen her and was behaving oddly, Polonius concluded that Hamlet's madness was due to Ophelia's rejection of his love. Nevertheless, the king was not convinced by Polonius' theory and continued to be wary of Hamlet.

A group of traveling actors arrived at court. Hamlet greeted them and asked them to recite lines from famous plays. He was ashamed they were so **passionate**[8] about something that existed only in the imagination, and blamed himself for not taking revenge for an actual wrong. Hamlet instructed them to add a scene in the play they would perform for the court. It would show a king murdered by his nephew who poured poison into his ears. Hamlet hoped a guilty response from his uncle to his "mousetrap" would confirm the ghost was telling the truth. However, the prince was being indecisive* again, further postponing his revenge.

Words for Production

1. heir [ɛr] *n.* [C] 繼承人
2. resent [rɪ`zɛnt] *v.* 感到憤恨；不滿
3. disclose [dɪs`kloz] *v.* 表明，透露
4. foul [faʊl] *adj.* 邪惡的；殘忍的
5. paralyze [`pærə,laɪz] *v.* 使麻痺
6. suspicious [sə`spɪʃəs] *adj.* 懷疑的
7. disapprove [,dɪsə`pruv] *v.* 反對
8. passionate [`pæʃənɪt] *adj.*
   情緒激昂的，熱情的

Words for Recognition

* coronation [,kɔrə`neʃən] *n.* [C]
  加冕典禮
* indecisive [,ɪndɪ`saɪsɪv] *adj.*
  優柔寡斷的，猶豫不決的

Idioms and Phrases

1. creep up on sb 從身後靠近…
2. blame sb/sth for sth
   把…歸咎於；責怪…

Something You Should Know

哈姆雷特為了測試叔父是否為殺父凶手，安排了一場戲，找來一個巡迴的演藝團到皇宮中演出類似的劇情。這段情節置入主戲之中，稱為「戲中戲」(the play within the play)，莎士比亞在《馴悍記》(*The Taming of the Shrew*)、《亨利四世上集》(*Henry IV, Part I*) 等劇中也用了這個手法。在此劇中，這個場景稱為「捕鼠器」(The Mousetrap)，意思是為了逮住真凶而設的陷阱。

Discussion

Do you agree with the ancient practice of "vendetta," meaning a son should avenge his father's murder? And, do you sympathize with Hamlet's situation?

Before the performance, Hamlet plunged into despair. He asked himself, "To be or not to be, that is the question," meaning that he was contemplating suicide. Hamlet was pondering a grim choice. Should he simply put an end to his "sea of troubles" by killing himself? Alternatively*, should he struggle to overcome them? He decided the former was no solution because death was an "undiscovered country." He feared he would journey to an after-life as dreadful as his present existence.

Hence, Hamlet attended the play. After the murder scene, Claudius called for "lights" and rushed away. Hamlet was now certain of his uncle's guilt. The king also knew Hamlet was a danger to him. The scene had mirrored how he had murdered his brother, but also contained a veiled* threat because Hamlet had the nephew kill his uncle.

Claudius decided to send Hamlet away on a diplomatic mission to England, where he planned to have him killed. He summoned Rosencrantz and Guildenstern. They were old friends of Hamlet now employed by the king. Claudius was using them to spy on Hamlet. He told them to prepare to sail to England with the prince.

When they left, the king suddenly suffered from a **bout**[9] of guilt. He knelt down to pray for forgiveness. Hamlet entered the hall and saw him at prayer, but failed to act. He convinced himself that his uncle would go to heaven if he killed him when he was praying. Hamlet wished to **condemn**[10] him to hell, so he spared him and left. However, Claudius then ceased praying because he realized he would never alter his own evil nature.

Later, Hamlet visited his mother in her chamber. There, Polonius was advising her to control her son. When he heard Hamlet, he hid behind a curtain. Hamlet intended to tell the queen about his father's murder. However, when she was frightened by his anger, Polonius shouted for help. Hamlet recklessly thrust his sword through the curtain, killing the councilor. He had **assumed**[11] it was the king. The ghost now reappeared to Hamlet alone and blamed him for **neglecting**[12] his vow.

When the king discovered Polonius had been killed, he insisted Hamlet leave for England at once. He lied to Rosencrantz and Guildenstern, claiming it was necessary to protect Hamlet from public anger over Polonius' death. However, in the letter he gave them for the English king, he requested the monarch to execute Hamlet.

When Hamlet was about to **embark**[13], he encountered a captain from the Norwegian army. The soldier announced that he was seeking permission for Prince Fortinbras and his army to cross Danish territory to Poland. Fortinbras had quarreled with the Polish king over a trivial piece of disputed land and was determined to fight him for it. On hearing this, Prince Hamlet was again furious with himself, for he had done nothing despite having much stronger motivation for action than his royal **counterpart**[14].

When Hamlet was away, Polonius' son, Laertes, returned from his studies in France. He sought swift revenge for his father's death. Claudius met him and claimed he was innocent of killing Polonius. Then, Laertes' sister, Ophelia, appeared in a terrible condition. She had gone mad because of the **trauma**[15] of her father's death and Hamlet's behavior. Laertes wanted immediate revenge and Claudius promised him justice.

Something You Should Know

"To be or not to be, that is the question." 可以說是莎士比亞名句中的名句，點出哈姆雷特深沉的困境與困惑，數百年來也觸動無數莎迷靈魂深處對生命與生存處境的迷惘。哈姆雷特的悲劇性格源自他的猶豫不決，讓自己陷入一個沒有行動只有反覆雜念的困境。「活著」或者「自殺」是他兩難的抉擇，活著要忍受無盡的苦難；選擇死亡又恐懼於未知的死後世界；未知，是因為從來沒有死去的人能夠回來告訴我們死後的種種。哈姆雷特沒有瘋，但是瘋人卻沒有他這麼坐困愁城。

Words for Production

9. bout [baut] *n.* [C] 一陣，一場
10. condemn [kən`dɛm] *v.* 宣判；判處（某人某種刑罰）
11. assume [ə`sum] *v.* 假定，假設
12. neglect [nɪ`glɛkt] *v.* 忽視，疏忽
13. embark [ɪm`bark] *v.* 上船
14. counterpart [`kauntɚ͵part] *n.* [C] 職位（或作用）相當的人；相對應的事物
15. trauma [`traumə] *n.* [C][U] 精神創傷

Words for Recognition

* alternatively [ɔl`tɝnətɪvlɪ] *adv.* 或者

* veiled [veld] *adj.* 不明言的；含蓄的

Idioms and Phrases

3. plunge into sth 突然變得⋯；陷入⋯
4. quarrel with sb over sth 與⋯為⋯爭吵

Discussion

When faced with a dilemma, killing his uncle to avenge his father's murder by his uncle, Hamlet hesitates. Would you feel the same way as Hamlet does? Why?

The king was shocked to receive news that Hamlet was returning. It meant his plan had failed. Hamlet had opened the letter carried by Rosencrantz and Guildenstern and discovered Claudius' plot to **assassinate**[16] him. Then, the ship was attacked by **pirates**[17]. Hamlet was captured but persuaded them to take him back to Denmark* where he would reward them.

Laertes demanded to fight Hamlet. His **fury**[18] increased when he learned of his sister's death because of her grief. Claudius persuaded Laertes to let him arrange Hamlet's death, for the prince was popular with the people who would disapprove of Laertes killing him. Laertes listened to the king's plot and agreed to assist him.

Claudius sent a servant to invite Hamlet to a fencing contest with Laertes. He told Hamlet that the king had bet Hamlet would win. Because it was a public contest and only **blunt**[19] swords could be used, Hamlet did not suspect anything. However, Laertes' sword had poison on its tip. He would pretend to thrust too hard by accident and cut Hamlet. The king had also prepared a cup of poisoned wine for Hamlet to drink during the match.

Thus, Hamlet and Laertes began to fight. During a pause in the contest, the queen offered Hamlet his drink. He refused, wishing to win quickly. Disaster struck when the queen herself sipped the wine before Claudius could prevent her. Meanwhile, Laertes and Hamlet fought closely and Laertes stabbed Hamlet. However, their weapons were exchanged while they wrestled and Hamlet accidentally cut Laertes with the poisoned sword.

The queen cried out because she was dying from the effects of the poisoned drink. She fell down dead. The dying Laertes then told the injured Hamlet about Claudius' plot. With his remaining strength, Hamlet wounded the king with the poisoned sword. He also forced him to drink from the poisoned cup. Claudius dropped dead next to the queen. Laertes and Hamlet forgave each other before they too **expired**[20].

Finally, Prince Fortinbras entered the court on his way back from his successful war in Poland*. Observing the chaos, he claimed the throne of Denmark, since all the royal family were dead. Nevertheless, he was sorry that Hamlet had died in this tragic way as he believed he would have made a good king. Therefore, he ordered Hamlet to be honored with a full military funeral.

Something You Should Know

奧菲莉亞是丹麥王國老臣之女，原與哈姆雷特互有愛意。哈姆雷特出國留學期間突遭家變，匆忙回國，卻使得兩人戀情生變。哈姆雷特裝瘋，奧菲莉亞的父親要她利用兩人的情誼前往刺探，致使她遭到多疑敏感的哈姆雷特羞辱。在「戲中戲」演出完畢之時，新王露出破綻，母后大驚失色，哈姆雷特頓時百感交集，怒急攻心，再度對奧菲莉亞厲言相向。奧菲莉亞經此巨變後得了失心瘋，於河邊行走時失足落水溺斃。奧菲莉亞在劇中是一個溫柔婉約的弱女子，聽命於父親，成為被物化的工具，再被所愛的男子肆意侮辱，最後的死亡也不具積極的意義。她在莎劇和文學史上的意象是一個父權文化的犧牲品。

Words for Production

16. assassinate [əˋsæsn͵et] *v.* 暗殺，行刺
17. pirate [ˋpaɪrət] *n.* [C] 海盜
18. fury [ˋfjʊrɪ] *n.* [U] *sing.* 暴怒，狂怒
19. blunt [blʌnt] *adj.* 鈍的，不鋒利的
20. expire [ɪkˋspaɪr] *v.* 逝世，亡故

Words for Recognition

* Denmark [ˋdɛnmɑrk] *n.* 丹麥
* Poland [ˋpolənd] *n.* 波蘭

Idioms and Phrases

5. agree to do sth
   應允…，答應…，同意…
6. pretend to do sth 假裝…

Discussion

The court of Denmark is finally rid of evil forces such as murder and killing. This is a typical resolution which restores order to the Shakespearean tragedies. Do you think that by doing this Shakespeare reflects the truth of the real world?

一、閱讀測驗 (Reading Comprehension)

1. What did Hamlet do to confirm that his uncle had killed his father?

   (A) He added a scene in the play that was going to be performed in court.

   (B) He sent one of his most trustworthy guards to monitor his uncle closely.

   (C) He met his uncle in person and demanded that his uncle tell him the truth.

   (D) He put great efforts into collecting related evidence and information.

2. What did Hamlet mean by saying "To be or not to be, that is the question?"

   (A) He felt like killing his uncle as soon as possible and becoming the king.

   (B) He was suffering from great agony and considered ending his own life.

   (C) He longed to marry Ophelia and live a blissful life with her forever.

   (D) He was determined to confront Claudius and ask him some questions.

3. According to this story, which of the following statements is true about Hamlet?

   (A) He didn't have any chance to kill his uncle before fighting with Laertes.

   (B) He was informed of the truth of his father's death by his friend Horatio.

   (C) He once became insane because of Ophelia's rejection of his strong love.

   (D) He revenged his father by forcing his uncle to drink a poisoned cup.

4. What lesson can we learn from Hamlet's tragedy?

   (A) The death of both parents is considered one of the biggest tragedies in life.

   (B) The life of royal family is always filled with murders and conspiracies.

   (C) One should be resolute in taking action when faced with a tough situation.

   (D) When we experience a sense of guilt, we should pray to God for forgiveness.

二、字彙填充 (Fill in the Blanks)

_____ 1. Legend has it that some p_____es buried their treasures in this island.

_____ 2. The news that the brave firefighter had e_____ed made people grieve.

_____ 3. Lucas is so p_____e about NBA that he watches every game on TV.

三、引導式翻譯 (Guided Translation)

1. Peter 責怪自己沒有準時交出作業。

   Peter _____ himself _____ not handing in the assignment on time.

2. Kelly 和她老公常常為了瑣碎的小事與對方爭吵。

   Kelly and her husband often _____ _____ each other _____ trivial things.

3. David 總是假裝自己對這個社區很熟悉。

   David always _____ _____ be very familiar with this community.

賞析

　　莎士比亞的四大悲劇 (*Hamlet*、*King Lear*、*Macbeth* 和 *Othello*) 都圍繞著一個人生的難題和謎題：事與願違。《哈姆雷特》的悲劇糾結於他的復仇使命、懷疑鬼魂的真實性、懷疑母親的貞潔和女友的真情，最終也懷疑自己的判斷與存在的價值。

　　生命的意義在於實現自己的潛能，為自己和周遭的人創造幸福，也在於感受到自己存在的意義，以及肯定自己所愛的人也受益於自己的付出。但是，哈姆雷特在這些方面都沒有成功。他花費許多時間去「確定」太多他認為可疑的事，以致於行動受到拖延。最為關鍵的一幕就是，他雖懷疑叔父謀害父親，但是當叔父獨處一室跪地禱告之時，他本可輕易下手，完成傳統認為兒子該替父親報仇的責任（家族世仇稱為 vendetta），他卻以死於禱告之際的惡人可能上天堂的民間說法為理由，而沒有作為，錯失良機。他雖愛奧菲莉亞，卻以尖刻的語言斥責她，令她發瘋溺水而亡。拖延與懷疑是他的兩大心魔（或稱為 "tragic flaw" 悲劇性格），最終也導致自己的死亡。

　　哈姆雷特的故事起源於一則西元十三世紀作家薩克索・格拉瑪提庫斯 (Saxo Grammaticus) 以拉丁文寫成的丹麥王子阿姆雷特 (Amleth) 的復仇故事，出版於 1514 年。學者認為莎士比亞讀到了 1570 年出版的這個故事的法文版，作者為弗朗西斯・迪・貝勒弗萊斯特 (François de Belleforest)。這個故事與《哈姆雷特》有許多雷同之處，包括王子的身分、父親、叔父與母親的三角關係、王子裝瘋、誤殺老臣等細節，但莎士比亞把原劇的圓滿結局改寫為悲劇。改寫的理由也有學者臆測，可能與莎士比亞寫作此劇時恰逢父病，繼而喪子（名為 Hamnet）有關，可能莎翁刻意將原劇主角的名字改為 Hamlet，用以紀念自己的兒子。但是，這個論點並無實證。

　　《哈姆雷特》一劇以謀殺開始，以決鬥誤傷毒發死亡結束，可以說是徹頭徹尾的悲劇。學者常指出，莎翁的悲劇在黑暗的盡頭總是安排一個秩序的恢復。此劇結尾挪威王子福丁布拉斯 (Fortinbras) 帶兵到達腐敗死寂的丹麥宮廷繼承王位重整秩序，猶如人生盛衰的興替，惡最終會由善來取代。這或許是悲劇引人入勝的原因：亞里斯多德 (Aristotle) 認為悲劇有精神淨化的作用 (catharsis)，觀眾／讀者在結束時流下同情之淚，暫時擱置對人生難題與謎題的不解，以淚水洗去心裡對好人遭遇乖戾命運的不捨與惶惑，走出劇院再度勇敢面對真實的人生。莎士比亞通透人性，與古希臘悲劇——《伊底帕斯王》(*Oedipus Rex*) 所開創的傳統可說一脈相承。

　　悲劇是一種文類 (genre)，相對於喜劇的嬉鬧與歡樂，它處理的是深沉的人生存在的意義的哲理議題。劇中的曠世名句「生存還是毀滅 "To be or not to be"」透過哈姆雷特說出，確實觸動了普世的人心。人的生存價值何在？為一己而活，或為責任而活？莎士比亞藉由哈姆雷特的悲劇人生，探索了生命的意義。哈姆雷特的主題提供了讀者生命教育的素材，讓讀者去反思生命的複雜性與重要性。

Chapter 5 *Pride and Prejudice*

關於作者

　　珍‧奧斯汀 (Jane Austen, 1775–1817) 出生於英國南部史帝文頓 (Steventon) 小鎮，父親是當地的牧師，也私辦寄宿小學，教育富裕家庭的男孩，一方面傳揚自己的教育理念，同時也為貼補家計。奧斯汀從小與六個兄長和一個姊姊在家由父親親自教導，沒有進過正規學校。家人一起讀書討論，說、寫孩童和青少年感興趣的故事。多年耳濡目染之下，奧斯汀十多歲開始寫作，題材包括人物速寫、搞笑短劇和短篇探險故事等。尚未成年的她已匿名完成《第一印象》(*First Impressions*) 的手稿，雖有兄長代她向出版商探意，但未獲青睞，只好先行擱置。倒是第二本小說《理性與感性》(*Sense and Sensibility*) 卻先於 1811 年出版。這時，因當時另一位女作家芬尼‧柏妮 (Fanny Burney) 新出版的小說剛好也以《第一印象》為書名，奧斯汀於是將自己經過數度修改的小說《第一印象》改名為《傲慢與偏見》(*Pride and Prejudice*)，於 1813 年出版，是她六本小說中最受讀者歡迎、流傳久遠的經典作品。

　　奧斯汀共出版六本小說：《理性與感性》(1811)，《傲慢與偏見》(1813)，《曼斯菲爾德莊園》(*Mansfield Park*) (1814)，《愛瑪》(*Emma*) (1816)，《諾桑覺寺》(*Northanger Abbey*) (1817) 和《說服》(*Persuasion*) (1817)，後兩者在她死後才出版。奧斯汀一生靦腆不喜社交，只與家人親近，與姊姊卡珊卓 (Cassandra) 尤其形影不離。雖然如此，但她博覽群書，享有優質的家庭教育和親情，加以近親和遠親都屬有聲望地位的人，因此她的小說無不流露對社會現況的瞭解與針砭，以及突顯人性在社會脈絡中磨練而成的尊嚴或淪喪而致的低鄙。奧斯汀的故事圍繞家庭倫理，作為敘事架構的主軸，學者常稱她的文體為家庭小說 (domestic fiction)。

珍‧奧斯汀年表

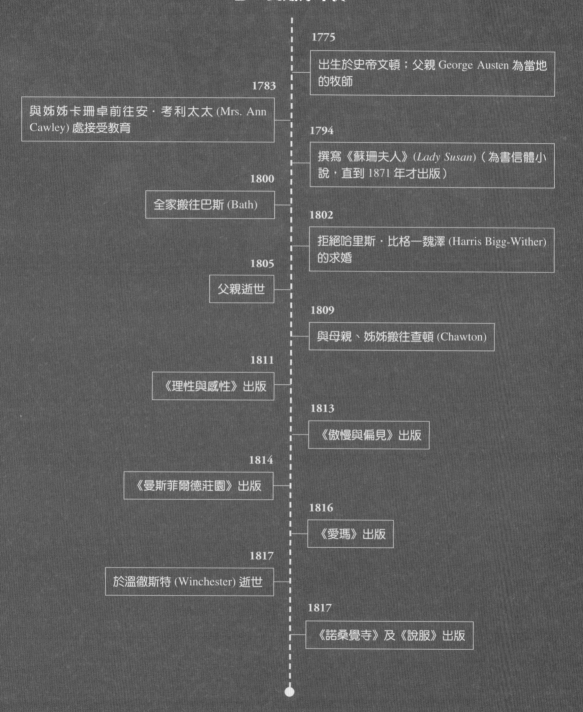

1775
出生於史帝文頓；父親 George Austen 為當地的牧師

1783
與姊姊卡珊卓前往安‧考利太太 (Mrs. Ann Cawley) 處接受教育

1794
撰寫《蘇珊夫人》(*Lady Susan*)（為書信體小說，直到 1871 年才出版）

1800
全家搬往巴斯 (Bath)

1802
拒絕哈里斯‧比格─魏澤 (Harris Bigg-Wither) 的求婚

1805
父親逝世

1809
與母親、姊姊搬往查頓 (Chawton)

1811
《理性與感性》出版

1813
《傲慢與偏見》出版

1814
《曼斯菲爾德莊園》出版

1816
《愛瑪》出版

1817
於溫徹斯特 (Winchester) 逝世

1817
《諾桑覺寺》及《說服》出版

When the wealthy **bachelor**[1] Charles Bingley rented the **estate**[2] of Netherfield Park, Mrs. Bennet was very excited. The Bennet family lived in the neighboring estate of Longbourn. She hoped he would marry one of her five daughters.

Mrs. Bennet wished her daughters to marry well because her husband's estate was entailed*. This meant Longbourn would be **inherited**[3] by the closest male relative. Mrs. Bennet feared her daughters' dependence on the goodwill of the male heir. She was delighted when a ball* was arranged in the nearby village of Meryton because Mr. Bingley would be attending. He arrived accompanied by a wealthy friend, Mr. Fitzwilliam Darcy.

During the evening, Mr. Bingley's friendly nature made him popular. However, Mr. Darcy was disliked for his proud manner. Mr. Bingley was attracted to the Bennets' eldest daughter, Jane. He encouraged his friend to dance with Jane's pretty younger sister, Elizabeth. Mr. Darcy said that she was "not handsome enough to tempt me." **Overhearing**[4] their conversation, Elizabeth was convinced Mr. Darcy was an **arrogant**[5] and unpleasant man.

Mrs. Bennet was pleased when Jane received an invitation from Mr. Bingley's sisters to spend a day at Netherfield while the gentlemen dined with officers from a military unit staying in Meryton. Mrs. Bennet decided to send her daughter on horseback, not in the carriage. She hoped that it would rain. Jane would then have to stay overnight at Netherfield and therefore meet Mr. Bingley again. Mrs. Bennet's plan worked. It rained and Jane got wet. However, she also caught a serious cold and had to stay a few days. Mrs. Bennet sent Elizabeth to look after her.

During this period Mr. Bingley and Jane grew more attached. Unknown to Elizabeth, Mr. Darcy was also becoming attracted to her. He admired her independence and intelligence. When she refused to dance with him one evening because of her wounded pride at the Meryton ball, his respect for her independent character grew.

After the Bennet sisters returned to Longbourn, the family was visited by Mr. Bennet's cousin Mr. William Collins, the heir to the estate. He was on his way to a new church appointment. Mr. Collins had been made rector* of the parish* of Lady Catherine de Bourgh, who was also Mr. Darcy's aunt. Elizabeth considered Mr. Collins a proud and ridiculous man. His main reason for visiting was to use his social status to select one of the Bennet sisters as his wife.

The day after his arrival, Mr. Collins accompanied the sisters on a trip to Meryton. There they encountered an officer who was friendly with the Bennets' two youngest daughters, Catherine and Lydia. He introduced them to Mr. George Wickham, who had just joined the unit. The sisters all liked the charming, handsome officer. Then Mr. Bingley and Mr. Darcy rode down the street and greeted the party. Elizabeth noticed that Mr. Wickham and Mr. Darcy acted very coldly towards each other.

On **subsequent**[6] meetings, Elizabeth became fond of Mr. Wickham. She asked him about Mr. Darcy. Mr. Wickham said his father had been the **steward**[7] of Pemberley, Mr. Darcy's late father's estate. He said that Mr. Darcy's father had treated him like another son and promised him a property with an income, but that Mr. Darcy refused to give it to him after his father's death. Mr. Wickham claimed that Mr. Darcy had been jealous of his father's **affection**[8] for him. His account strengthened Elizabeth's hostility towards Mr. Darcy.

Something You Should Know

　　十八世紀英國小説家之中有許多是女性，寫作的題材常是女性所關心的感情與婚姻等，尤其有關女性的社會障礙以及女性的主體性。班奈特家有五個女兒，沒有兒子，在法律上女兒不能繼承家產，要由男性親戚繼承，於是故事中班奈特家面臨迫在眉睫的危機就是未來的生計問題。英國傳統上實施「長子繼承制」(primogeniture)，家中若有兄弟，所有祖產由長子繼承，次子以降和女兒都無權繼承。這個制度根深蒂固，衍生出很多社會問題。

單字朗讀 **完整** MP3 Ch5 Vocabulary

Words for Production

1. bachelor [`bætʃələ] *n.* [C] 未婚男子
2. estate [ə`stet] *n.* [C]（位於鄉村的）大片私有土地，莊園
3. inherit [ɪn`hɛrɪt] *v.* 繼承
4. overhear [ˌovə`hɪr] *v.* 無意中聽到
5. arrogant [`ærəgənt] *adj.* 傲慢的
6. subsequent [`sʌbsɪˌkwɛnt] *adj.* 隨後的，接著的
7. steward [`stjuwəd] *n.* [C] 服務員
8. affection [ə`fɛkʃən] *n.* [U] *sing.* 喜愛

Words for Recognition

* entail [ɪn`tel] *v.* 限定繼承；遺留給…
* ball [bɔl] *n.* [C] 舞會
* rector [`rɛktə] *n.* [C] 教區長，教區牧師
* parish [`pærɪʃ] *n.* [C] 行政教區

Idioms and Phrases

1. look after sb 照顧…，看管…

Discussion

In traditional societies worldwide, unmarried women over a certain age are called "spinsters" or other names with a bad connotation. What about today? Do you see a change in our society?

Mr. Collins was initially attracted to Jane until he heard that she was likely to marry Mr. Bingley. He then proposed to Elizabeth, certain she would accept. However, she politely but firmly rejected him on personal grounds, saying they were not suitable for each other. Mrs. Bennet was furious. She believed her daughter should marry the heir to the estate for the sake of the Bennet family's future. Mr. Collins later proposed to Elizabeth's best friend Charlotte who lived near Meryton. She accepted him because Mr. Collins would bring her financial security.

Mrs. Bennet was further disappointed when Mr. Bingley had to leave for London on business. Soon afterwards Mrs. Bennet's brother, Mr. Gardiner, came to visit with his wife. They invited Jane to stay with them in London. Elizabeth hoped she would meet Mr. Bingley there. Mrs. Gardiner noticed Elizabeth's attraction to Mr. Wickham. She was suspicious, warning her that he was too poor and it would not be sensible for her to marry him. However, Elizabeth was determined not to be **prejudiced**[9] against him for his lack of wealth.

A few weeks later, Elizabeth received a letter from Jane in London. She wrote that she had called on Miss Bingley but was not made welcome. Jane believed that Miss Bingley wished her brother to marry Mr. Darcy's sister because she was wealthier and thus wanted to prevent her meeting Mr. Bingley.

In March, Charlotte's parents, Sir William and Lady Lucas, invited Elizabeth on a northern tour. On their way they visited their daughter and her husband, Mr. Collins, in his parish. While there, they dined with Lady Catherine de Bourgh at Rosings Park, her country **mansion**[10]. Mr. Darcy was also visiting his aunt. Elizabeth and Mr. Darcy met socially*, but she was not friendly towards him.

Therefore, she was surprised when Mr. Darcy suddenly proposed. She calmly refused him. However, she became angry when Mr. Darcy admitted it was he who had prevented Jane and Mr. Bingley from meeting in London. He believed Jane's background was not good enough for his friend. **Annoyed**[11] by his social prejudice, Elizabeth then accused him of cheating Mr. Wickham. Mr. Darcy did not answer and left.

The next day Elizabeth **encountered**[12] Mr. Darcy on a walk. He gave her a letter and walked away. It stated that his father had left Mr. Wickham a thousand pounds and the promise of an appointment in the church. However, Mr. Wickham was not interested in this career and asked Mr. Darcy for an extra two thousand pounds instead. He soon wasted the money. Mr. Darcy then explained he had to prevent Mr. Wickham from running away with his younger sister to marry her for her wealth. Elizabeth's feelings towards Mr. Darcy were now confused and she realized she might have been mistaken* to trust Mr. Wickham.

Something You Should Know

　　故事中提到達西先生一共給了韋克翰三千鎊。當時一名牧師年薪不到三百鎊，可見達西先生的寬厚慷慨。達西為人木訥，不擅長自我表白，於是寫了信告訴伊莉莎白事情的真相。當時的小說家喜歡用書信做為說故事的方法，一方面描摹人物的性格，另一方面也提供讀者學習如何寫信，可以當作一種「尺牘大全」，讓讀者感覺有額外的收穫。在奧斯汀之前，英國小說名家理查森 (Samuel Richardson) 更擅長這個技巧，所著《克拉麗莎‧哈洛》(Clarissa Harlowe) 和《潘蜜拉》(Pamela) 用了大量的書信來抒情與敘事，是「書信體小說」(epistolary novel) 著名的例子。

Words for Production

9. prejudiced [`prɛdʒədɪsd] *adj.* 有偏見的

10. mansion [`mænʃən] *n.* [C] 大廈；豪宅

11. annoy [ə`nɔɪ] *v.* 煩擾；打擾；使煩惱

12. encounter [ɪn`kaʊntɚ] *v.* 邂逅，不期而遇，偶然碰到

Words for Recognition

* socially [`soʃəlɪ] *v.* 社交方面的；與社交場合有關的
* mistaken [mə`stekən] *adj.* 判斷錯誤的；被誤解的

Idioms and Phrases

2. for the sake of sth 因…的緣故

3. call on sb 拜訪；訪問

4. accuse sb of sth 控告…；控訴…

Discussion

First impressions are often deceptive. Other than Elizabeth and Darcy, misled by their wrong impressions of each other when they first meet, do you find another example of such first impression? Describe the details.

When Elizabeth returned to Longbourn, she told Jane about Mr. Wickham, but they decided not to make the information public. Meanwhile, Mr. Wickham's unit was posted to Brighton. The wife of Colonel Forster in the unit invited Lydia Bennet to spend the summer in Brighton. Lydia was excited to be able to keep meeting the officers. Her father gave his permission, believing the colonel and his wife would supervise her properly.

In July, Elizabeth went on a trip to Derbyshire with the Gardiners. They passed Pemberley, Mr. Darcy's country house. Believing him away, they took a tour of the estate. Elizabeth wondered what it would be like to live there as Mr. Darcy's wife. They chatted to Mr. Darcy's housekeeper, who said he treated the people on his estate very well.

Then, Mr. Darcy suddenly* appeared. He had returned to prepare the house for guests. He invited them all to dinner the following day. Mrs. Gardiner noticed that Mr. Darcy was in love with Elizabeth. When Elizabeth returned to the inn she was staying at, she received letters from Jane. They said that Lydia had run away with Mr. Wickham.

Mr. Gardiner and Mr. Bennet travelled to London to search for the couple. Mr. Gardiner eventually found them. Mr. Wickham insisted that Mr. Bennet **guarantee**[13] him an income before he married Lydia. Mr. Bennet agreed in order to save his family's **reputation**[14]. Later, Mrs. Gardiner informed Elizabeth that Mr. Darcy had also paid Mr. Wickham a large sum. Elizabeth was moved by his **generosity**[15] and regretted her refusal to marry him.

Finally, Mr. Bingley returned to Netherfield. He visited Longbourn and stayed for dinner. A few days later, he proposed to Jane and she accepted. Meanwhile, Elizabeth received a surprise visit from Lady Catherine de Bourgh. She suspected that Mr. Darcy

was in love with her, and wanted to prevent their marriage. She said that Elizabeth's social status made her an unsuitable* match for her nephew. Elizabeth refused to be influenced and told her she had the right to choose who she wanted to marry.

A few days later Mr. Darcy visited Netherfield. Mr. Bingley took him to visit the Bennets at Longbourn. On a walk Elizabeth thanked Mr. Darcy for helping Lydia, and revealed her change of opinion about his character. Mr. Darcy proposed again and this time she agreed to marry him. Thus, Jane and Elizabeth were happily married. Elizabeth went to live at Pemberley. Mr. Bingley **purchased**[16] a property nearby and the sisters were able to visit each other frequently. Mrs. Bennet was, of course, delighted.

Something You Should Know

　　小說家在虛構的情節中常會加入自己的成長經驗，奧斯汀也不例外。小說中兩位女主角的姐妹情彷彿作者的自傳。整個故事舖陳了許多波折，尤其是伊莉莎白與達西先生之間，內在的誤會偏見以及外在的阻力，延宕了他們的快樂結局。奧斯汀突顯他們的人品，正直、擇善固執和勇於認錯。她以喜劇的結尾表達善有善報的信念，如伊莉莎白與達西先生、賓利與珍的善良，克服了當時英國社會階級與性別偏見，終得幸福。兩位女主角的圓滿結局可視為奧斯汀自己願望的投射。

Words for Production

13. guarantee [ˌɡærənˈti] *v.* 確保
14. reputation [ˌrɛpjəˈteʃən] *n.* [C][U] 名聲；聲望；名望
15. generosity [ˌdʒɛnəˈrɑsətɪ] *n.* [U] 慷慨
16. purchase [ˈpɝtʃəs] *v.* 購買

Words for Recognition

* suddenly [ˈsʌdənlɪ] *adv.* 突然；驟然
* unsuitable [ʌnˈsutəbl̩] *adj.* 不適宜的

Idioms and Phrases

5. run away with sb 與⋯私奔

Discussion

In what ways does this novel appeal to you? Who among the main characters do you like the most, and why?

一、閱讀測驗 (Reading Comprehension)

1. In this story, when parents were choosing husbands for their daughters, what were their primary considerations?

    (A) Social status and wealth.

    (B) Personality and education.

    (C) Intelligence and abilities.

    (D) Appearances and stature.

2. What's Elizabeth's first impression of Mr. Darcy?

    (A) She thought he was a friendly and polite gentleman.

    (B) She thought he was a conceited and unpleasant man.

    (C) She thought he was the most suitable man for her.

    (D) She thought he was a handsome and intelligent man.

3. Which of the following relationships between characters is **NOT** true?

    (A) Charlotte was Elizabeth's best friend.

    (B) Lady Catherine de Bourgh was Darcy's aunt.

    (C) George Wickham was Charles Bingley's cousin.

    (D) Mrs. Bennet was Catherine and Lydia's mother.

4. Which of the following statements regarding Elizabeth is true?

    (A) She was never really fond of Mr. Wickham.

    (B) All she wanted was marry a wealthy gentleman.

    (C) She accepted Darcy's first proposal on the spot.

    (D) She was an intelligent and independent woman.

二、字彙填充 (Fill in the Blanks)

_____ 1. Paul is so a_____t and selfish that no one wants to make friends with him.

_____ 2. Richard's new m_____n is estimated at more than ten million dollars.

_____ 3. Many people are accustomed to p_____sing most daily necessities online.

三、引導式翻譯 (Guided Translation)

1. Helen 和她的男朋友私奔了，這讓她的父母親感到很生氣。

    Helen _____ _____ _____ her boyfriend, which made her parents feel furious.

2. 這個年輕人被指控對人行道上的一排機車縱火。

    This young man _____ _____ _____ setting fire to a row of scooters on the sidewalk.

3. Sophia 為了那個老先生的龐大的財富而嫁給他。

    Sophia married the old man _____ _____ _____ _____ his great wealth.

賞析

《傲慢與偏見》的主要情節圍繞在兩位主角伊莉莎白和達西先生的戀情發展上，以及最後有情人終成眷屬的曲折過程。兩人之間的關係因誤解而導致達西先生表現傲慢、伊莉莎白懷抱偏見，直到最後逐漸化解誤會，成就良緣。伊莉莎白的姊姊珍和達西先生的好友賓利先生的姻緣則是一條陪襯的主題副線。雖然姊妹兩人生於中產階級的家庭，但最後破除當時社會根深蒂固的階級障礙，得以嫁給地主富紳，並與所愛的人廝守終身。

這對主角在戀愛路上的障礙主要來自兩人各自的性情偏差：初次見面時伊莉莎白相信自己對達西先生的負面判斷，達西先生則不喜伊莉莎白非貴族的家世以及平庸的雙親。這部小說原本想以《第一印象》(*First Impressions*) 為書名，但在出版之際已有剛出版的同名小說，因而改名，可見作者奧斯汀欲藉這個故事傳達主題：「拋棄成見，才能真心相愛。」兩人的阻力還來自當時英國社會的父權文化，體現在階級制度與男尊女卑的法律和習俗。班奈特家生有五個女兒，沒有兒子，父親對家人冷漠，只親近伊莉莎白，母親庸俗浮躁過日子的唯一目的就是盡速將五個女兒嫁掉，對賓利先生的家人和達西先生百般巴結，更令對方瞧不起。

奧斯汀寫作時的英國社會普遍認為「女子無才便是德」，唯一的歸宿就是婚姻和家庭生活。像故事中伊莉莎白的妹妹莉迪雅與男人私奔，被視為有虧婦道且有損家庭聲譽及個人名節。奧斯汀兄妹自小在家由父親教導學習，博覽群書，雖涉世不深，但書中知識廣袤，她得以綜覽人生百態，下筆自然充滿寫實的味道。加上兄妹感情和睦，互相切磋文采，也使得她的小說中洋溢手足之情，《傲慢與偏見》中伊莉莎白和珍的姊妹情誼便是真實人生中珍和姊姊卡珊卓 (Cassandra) 的寫照。

在子女眾多的家庭中，兄弟姊妹的親密情感和互動所在多有。奧斯汀的原生家庭注重家庭和知識教育，同胞手足的和諧互助與深厚情感最能體現家庭教育的成功。在這本小說中，伊莉莎白和珍的情感，前者聰慧伶俐，後者溫柔婉約，也在無形中成就了對方的美滿婚姻。另一個女兒也得到達西先生的協助，正式與她私奔的男子結婚，避免了一樁醜聞。全書終以喜劇結尾。

奧斯汀從小與父兄一起學習，沾染了陽剛文氣，善用機智語 (quick wit) 和反諷 (irony)，在小說中活用，例如全書開頭第一句便是：「"It is a truth universally acknowledged, that a single man in possession of a good fortune, must be in want of a wife."（一個有錢的單身漢必然缺個老婆，這是舉世皆然的真理。）」，讀者莞爾之餘更感受到作者的犀利與機智。如此文體和一般女性作家的閨秀風格大不相同，使得奧斯汀脫穎而出，在英國文學史上留下盛名。

Chapter 6　*Frankenstein*

關於作者

　　瑪麗·雪萊（Mary Shelley, 1797–1851，婚前姓名瑪麗·沃斯通克拉夫特·戈德溫）出生於 1797 年，父親是知名學者與思想家威廉·戈德溫 (William Godwin)，母親更是當時引領女權運動的作家瑪麗·沃斯通克拉夫特 (Mary Woolstonecraft)。兩人鼓吹人權和自由主義，與激進政治家湯瑪斯·潘恩 (Thomas Paine) 和特立獨行的詩人威廉·布雷克 (William Blake) 為朋儕密友。母親所著《女權辯護》(*A Vindication of the Rights of Woman*) 至今仍然擁有無數讀者，公認為是女權主義的巨作。母親因生她難產而去世，瑪麗由父親撫養長大。出身如此的家庭，瑪麗耳濡目染，一生行事獨立自主，文采斐然。

　　瑪麗於 1814 年初識文壇驕子珀西·比希·雪萊 (Percy Bysshe Shelley)，旋即陷入熱戀與他私奔，兩人攜手遊歷法國、瑞士和德國等地。瑪麗急欲逃離父親的管束，雪萊則為疏遠妻子哈莉葉 (Harriet)。雪萊與妻子關係時熱時冷，這個三角關係維持了兩年，到 1816 年冬天哈莉葉懷著身孕投河身亡。瑪麗與雪萊兩人選擇於兩週後結婚。

　　兩人的婚姻被人認為是愛情與文學的雙重結合。雪萊幫助瑪麗校訂《科學怪人》的初稿，並為這本小說操刀代寫作者自序。1818 年《科學怪人》出版，迅速成為暢銷書。兩人一共生育四個孩子，其中三個早夭。1822 年雪萊到義大利旅遊，不幸在托斯卡尼海邊因船隻沉沒而溺斃。此後，瑪麗獨自撫育孩子，在 1851 年辭世之前花費心力為雪萊編校出版他未完成的手稿，她自己也出版了另外五本小說。

瑪麗・雪萊年表

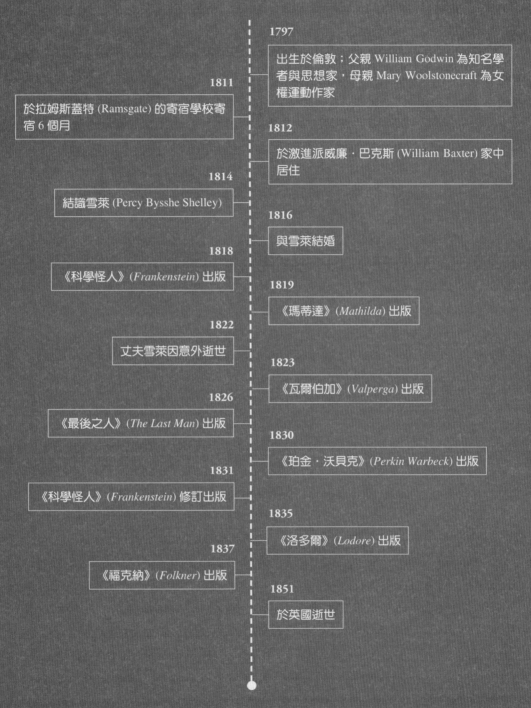

1797
出生於倫敦；父親 William Godwin 為知名學者與思想家，母親 Mary Woolstonecraft 為女權運動作家

1811
於拉姆斯蓋特 (Ramsgate) 的寄宿學校寄宿 6 個月

1812
於激進派威廉・巴克斯 (William Baxter) 家中居住

1814
結識雪萊 (Percy Bysshe Shelley)

1816
與雪萊結婚

1818
《科學怪人》(*Frankenstein*) 出版

1819
《瑪蒂達》(*Mathilda*) 出版

1822
丈夫雪萊因意外逝世

1823
《瓦爾伯加》(*Valperga*) 出版

1826
《最後之人》(*The Last Man*) 出版

1830
《珀金・沃貝克》(*Perkin Warbeck*) 出版

1831
《科學怪人》(*Frankenstein*) 修訂出版

1835
《洛多爾》(*Lodore*) 出版

1837
《福克納》(*Folkner*) 出版

1851
於英國逝世

An English explorer*, Robert Walton, was on an **expedition**[1] to the Arctic*. He wrote letters to his sister detailing his journey and its hardships. His fourth letter related some extraordinary and unexpected incidents.

His ship had become surrounded by ice. Walton saw an enormous figure in a sledge pulled by a pack of dogs. This creature was traveling fast to the north and soon disappeared from sight. In the evening, the ice broke up, freeing the ship. The next morning, he heard his sailors talking to a man on a sledge that had drifted on a sheet of ice towards their ship. Although the man was in terrible physical condition, he refused to board until he knew they were voyaging north. He told Walton he was pursuing the huge creature on the other sledge. Walton was impressed by the man's dignity and determination, considering him a "divine wanderer." The traveler asked Walton to listen to his story. Walton recorded it in a **manuscript**[2], which he sent to his sister.

The man, Victor Frankenstein, said he was born in Geneva, Switzerland. When his father's sister died, the family looked after her young daughter, Elizabeth. His mother hoped Victor might one day marry his cousin. His father then had two more sons. Victor also had a best friend, Henry Clerval. Victor developed an early interest in natural science. He was also enthusiastic about the ideas of ancient and medieval scientists who dreamed of summoning spirits or even creating life. He wanted to become a great scientist to benefit mankind. Victor was sent to study at the University of Ingolstadt in Germany. Just before he left, his mother became ill and died.

When he arrived in Ingolstadt, he met a professor who inspired him to master every branch of science. Victor believed the meeting decided his future destiny. He would study all night and do experiments. Then, Victor began to **speculate**[3] about the origin of life itself. He studied dead bodies and how they **decayed**[4]. During this time he made the amazing discovery of how to restore life to dead organic matter. He had the idea of creating a human being. Because it was difficult to **animate**[5] smaller body parts, Victor decided to construct a being of gigantic stature. He secretly collected large limbs and organs from **corpses**[6]

and built his creature in a laboratory in his house.

Finally, he used electricity to bring the creature to life. However, at the moment of his triumph, Victor realized that he had created a monster. The muscles and pumping blood vessels could be seen through the skin and the eyes were a horrible dull yellow color. Victor rushed out of the laboratory and, exhausted, fell asleep in his bedroom. He awoke to find the creature approaching his bed. Victor fled to the courtyard, hiding there until morning.

The next day, Victor hurried into the town. There he saw a coach that had come from Switzerland. His friend Henry Clerval stepped out. He had come to join Victor in Ingolstadt. Henry was shocked at how unwell Victor looked. Then, Victor fainted and was ill for months.

Something You Should Know

《科學怪人》的寫作背景是一則有趣的軼事。1816 年夏天，尚未成婚的瑪麗與雪萊到瑞士阿爾卑斯山麓遊歷，好友拜倫 (George Gordon Lord Byron) 同行。眾人被山中夏日少見的暴雨困在旅店裡無所事事，拜倫提議三人比賽，看看誰能快筆寫出最「驚悚」的鬼怪故事，用來排遣雨日的無聊。於是，有了瑪麗·雪萊寫成的《科學怪人》留傳後世。

單字朗讀 **完整** MP3 Ch6 Vocabulary

Words for Production

1. expedition [ˌɛkspɪ`dɪʃən] *n.* [C]
   遠征；探險，考察
2. manuscript [`mænjəˌskrɪpt] *n.* [C]
   手稿；原稿
3. speculate [`spɛkjəˌlet] *v.* 猜測；推測
4. decay [dɪ`ke] *v.* 腐蝕；衰敗
5. animate [`ænəˌmet] *v.* 使生氣勃勃
6. corpse [kɔrps] *n.* [C]
   （通常指人的）屍體

Words for Recognition

* explorer [ɪk`splorɚ] *n.* [C]
   探險家；勘探者；考察者
* the Arctic [`ɑktɪk] *n.* 北極，北極地區

Idioms and Phrases

1. a pack of . . . 一群…
2. step out 暫時離開

Discussion

Why do you think the author set the beginning of the story in the Arctic, an utmost wilderness seldom visited by humans? How does this device help convey the Gothic mood of the story?

When Victor recovered, he decided to return to Geneva*. He began to forget about the creature, which had disappeared. However, just before leaving for Switzerland, he received a letter from his father. The letter informed Victor that his youngest brother, William, had been murdered. His father found the little boy lying dead on the grass. Marks on his neck showed he had been **strangled**[7].

Victor immediately traveled to Geneva. Before he went home, he visited the site of the murder. It was night and there was a violent thunderstorm*. When he arrived, a flash of lightning **illuminated**[8] the figure of the creature, which then vanished into the night. Victor was convinced he was the killer.

Nevertheless, he knew no one would believe his story, so he remained silent. Then, the family's female servant Justine was accused of the crime. William always carried a small picture of his dead mother with him. It was discovered in Justine's pocket. Victor believed the creature had placed it there. Justine was found guilty and hanged. From that moment, Victor knew he would have a guilty **conscience**[9] forever, for by creating the creature he was "the true murderer." He resolved to find and destroy his creation.

One morning, Victor decided to climb a mountain alone because he didn't want his family to see how depressed he was. At the summit, he was approached by the creature. Victor attacked him but the creature easily avoided him. He then demanded that Victor listen to his story. The creature said he had wanted to be accepted by humanity. However, whenever people saw him, they ran away in terror and then hunted him. Consequently, he had to exist alone, living in wild places. In his isolation, he developed a hatred for mankind. He blamed Victor for creating and then abandoning him. Therefore, he took revenge on Victor's family. He wanted his creator to be equally miserable.

The creature demanded Victor end his **solitude**[10] by making him a wife like himself. He promised they would live apart from humanity and harm no one. Despite his evil deeds, Victor felt he was responsible for the creature's **welfare**[11] and agreed to his request. He also wished to protect people from his murderous anger. Victor had heard that some English scientists had knowledge that would help him build another creature more easily. He thus asked his father's permission to go to England with his friend Henry. Victor explained that he wanted a final trip before he settled down to marry Elizabeth.

In London, Victor obtained the information he required. Afterwards, Victor and Henry toured England and visited a friend in Scotland. Victor told Henry he wished to travel alone for a while and departed for a remote island off the north coast. There he rented a cottage and set up his laboratory. He collected body parts and began his work.

One evening the creature appeared at the laboratory window. He gave a horrible grin when he saw his half-finished female counterpart.

Victor saw the evil in his eyes and regretted his promise. He feared he would create two evil beings that would breed and threaten humanity. He tore the unfinished body to pieces. The creature gave "a **howl**[12] of devilish despair" and left with the menacing threat, "I shall be with you on your wedding-night."

Victor gathered the limbs and dumped them into the sea from a boat. He then fell asleep. He awoke to find he had drifted from the shore and was lost. Then, he suddenly spotted land. He had arrived in Ireland*. However, the locals were hostile and took him to the local judge.

Something You Should Know

哥德式小說是小說寫作的一種方法，起源於十八世紀英國，題材側重驚悚與暴力，因故事場景多為偏僻的尖聳幽暗哥德式古堡，因而得名。多數哥德式小說的主題不脫血腥和神祕力量，能夠吸引讀者進入迥異於真實人生的經驗，故而幾個世紀以來風行不斷。《科學怪人》加入科技原素，便成了哥德式科幻小說 (Gothic science fiction)，情節魔幻脫離現實，常取材自科學知識，但突顯虛構故事的寓意。

Words for Production

7. strangle [`stræŋgl̩] *v.* 勒死，掐死

8. illuminate [ɪ`lumə,net] *v.* 照亮

9. conscience [`kanʃəns] *n.* 良心，良知

10. solitude [`salɪ,tjud] *n.* [U] 孤獨，獨處

11. welfare [`wɛl,fɛr] *n.* [U]
（尤指人的）幸福，福祉；安康

12. howl [haʊl] *n.* [C] 號叫聲；喊叫聲

Words for Recognition

* Geneva [dʒə`nivə] *n.*
日內瓦（位於瑞士的城市）

* thunderstorm [`θʌndɚ,stɔrm] *n.* [C][U]
雷雨，雷暴

* Ireland [`aɪrlənd] *n.* 愛爾蘭島

Idioms and Phrases

3. take revenge on sb 報復…；報仇…

4. settle down （通常與伴侶）定居，安定下來

Discussion

Literary works very often move us profoundly because they deal with conflicts of various kinds. Can you describe the most compelling conflict you find in this novel?

課文朗讀 分段 MP3 Track 6-3

The judge told Victor he was suspected of murdering a man found on a nearby beach. Victor was shown the body and was **horrified**[13] to see it was of his friend Henry Clerval. He guessed the creature had done it. Victor was **imprisoned**[14] but was found not guilty. The evidence showed he was still on the island when his friend's body was found.

When Victor returned to Geneva, he married Elizabeth. If the creature attacked him on his wedding night, he was determined to fight him. The married couple stayed overnight at Evian on Lake Geneva. Armed with **pistols**[15] and a knife, Victor waited for the creature. Then, he heard a terrible scream from Elizabeth's room. He rushed in to find her lying dead, strangled by the creature. At the window he saw the creature, who grinned and **jeered**[16] as he pointed at Elizabeth. Victor fired his pistol, but the creature escaped.

When Victor's father heard the tragic news, he had a **stroke**[17] and died. Victor had a nervous **breakdown**[18]. After recovering, his only purpose in life was to kill the creature. He wandered all over the earth following his enemy, who took pleasure in his pursuit. Finally, he reached the Arctic and chased the creature until the ice broke and he was picked up by Walton's ship.

Something You Should Know

　　歐洲在中古世紀時期逐漸鞏固了基督教教會的威權體制，視教會為通往天堂的唯一途徑，全權代表上帝宰制教徒的命運，服從教會者得永生，違者入烈火焚身的地獄。這種教會中心論控制了信徒的思想和生活直至十五世紀文藝復興時期，人本思想逐漸萌芽，到了十八世紀之後，科學也逐漸興起。中古時期，煉金術被視為魔法，到了十八世紀，則被接納為化學科學，就是文明演進的一個例子。在這個科學興起的數百年期間，《聖經・創世記》描述的人類為上帝依祂的形象所造，成為神學與科學爭議的一大焦點。達爾文 (Charles Darwin) 的進化論 (Theory of Evolution) 主張人類是由猿猴演化而來，導致他被逐出教會。二十世紀後期盛行的宇宙大爆炸理論 (The Big Bang Theory) 提出了天地造物的科學版本。今天科學反過來成為人類生活與生命的支配者，而宗教則轉而成為唯心的意志修鍊方法與個人選擇的信仰，不再享有傳統教會的體制性威權。兩者似乎更強調協調平衡，而不是互不相容。

Walton wrote to his sister that Victor developed a fever and died soon after finishing his story. The sailors insisted that Walton sail to England because of the bad weather. When the ship had started the journey, Walton heard sounds from the cabin containing Victor's body. He discovered the creature **grieving**[19] over his creator's corpse.

The creature told Walton he now regretted his actions, but there was no one more miserable and lonely than himself on earth. He told Walton he would travel northwards* to die alone in the icy wastes. He then leaped out of the cabin window. Walton observed him speed away northwards on a **raft**[20], never to be seen again.

Words for Production

13. horrify [`hɔrə,faɪ] *v.* 使極為震驚；驚嚇
14. imprison [ɪm`prɪzn̩] *v.* 關押，囚禁
15. pistol [`pɪstl̩] *n.* [C] 手槍
16. jeer [dʒɪr] *v.* 嘲笑，嘲弄
17. stroke [strok] *n.* [C] 中風
18. breakdown [`brek,daʊn] *n.* [C]
    神經失常；神經衰弱
19. grieve [griv] *v.* （尤指為某人去世而）
    悲痛，悲傷，傷心
20. raft [ræft] *n.* [C] 筏；木筏

Words for Recognition

* northwards [`nɔrθwɚdz] *adv.* 向北地

Idioms and Phrases

5. armed with sth 備有…所需的
6. take pleasure in sth 愉快，歡樂

Discussion

Do you feel sympathy for the monster created by Victor Frankenstein? Why or why not?

一、閱讀測驗 (Reading Comprehension)

1. What's the main idea of this story?

    (A) A creature created by a scientist felt lonely and longed for a partner.

    (B) A young scientist regretted creating a creature and wanted to destroy it.

    (C) An ambitious scientist tried to create as many creatures as he could.

    (D) A horrible creature killed victims in a row and then vanished into thin air.

2. Which of the following was **NOT** murdered by the creature?

    (A) Elizabeth.

    (B) Walton.

    (C) William.

    (D) Henry.

3. What happened to the second creature that Victor had intended to create?

    (A) He later decided to ruin the unfinished body.

    (B) He couldn't find sufficient body parts to finish it.

    (C) He finished it and successfully brought it to life.

    (D) It broke down suddenly when he was about to finish it.

4. What can we infer about the creature that Victor created?

    (A) It didn't have any emotions such as love or hatred.

    (B) It took great pleasure in strangling people to death.

    (C) It was eager to learn how to create a creature like itself.

    (D) It actually didn't hate Victor and longed to be accepted by him.

二、字彙填充 (Fill in the Blanks)

_____ 1. There are a number of precious ancient m_____ts hidden in this cave.

_____ 2. The policeman drew his p_____l and fired several shots at the gangster.

_____ 3. Howard has been living in s_____e ever since his wife passed away.

三、引導式翻譯 (Guided Translation)

1. 那隻狐狸正被一群獵狗追捕著。

    The fox is being chased by _____ _____ _____ hounds.

2. Kevin 發誓要對那位殺害他妻子的人復仇。

    Kevin swore to _____ _____ _____ the man who had killed his wife.

3. 裝備著一把鋒利的劍和盾，那位英雄最後殺死了噴火龍。

    _____ _____ a sharp sword and a shield, the hero slaughtered the fire-breathing dragon at last.

賞析

　　《科學怪人》的故事主軸是維克多干犯禁忌，利用他的科學知識企圖「人造人」，僭越了上帝的角色，其行為也等同於施行邪魔妖術。除了這個宗教涵義之外，另外還有道德涵義：科學並非萬能，維克多掘墓盜屍加以縫補，利用科學賦予創造之「怪人」情感與語言能力，但仍無法使他成為一個真正的人類，融入社會享有人倫關係。維克多最終家破人亡，他自己要付全部的責任。從基督教的道統觀點（敬畏上帝，不逾越人的本分）來看，維克多是他所創造的那名「怪人」之外的另一個邪魔妖怪。

　　根據瑪麗在她 1831 年修訂版的簡介中說，書中最為驚悚的一幕就是「怪人」有了生命跡象，肢體開始出現動作時，那時的「怪人」外表恐怖至極，書中用的描述語是「像個邪魔鬼魅的人形(the hideous phantasm of a man)」。他所到之處引發驚恐，人人避之唯恐不及，「怪人」於挫折之餘，強烈要求維克多再造一個女性給他為伴，維克多也開始二度造人，但是臨成功之際卻生悔意，將半成品沉入湖中。「怪人」憤恨之餘謀害了維克多的新婚妻子。

　　《科學怪人》故事中有三個第一人稱說話人：華頓 (Robert Walton) 寫信給倫敦的妹妹，描述他如何搭救了維克多 (Victor Frankenstein)；接下來維克多說明他的遭遇；中間他也以第一人稱穿插「怪人」說的話。

　　瑪麗在這本小說的書名頁上引用了十七世紀詩人密爾頓 (John Milton) 鉅作《失樂園》(*Paradise Lost*) 中亞當的提問。亞當剛被逐出伊甸園，他問道：

　　造物主啊，我何曾請求祢以塵土

　　將我捏造為人，我何曾請求祢

　　將我從長夜之中拔擢而出（成為人）？（第十章 743–745 行）

亞當因為夏娃已吃了禁果，也跟著吃了，愛妻心切超出對上帝的服從，因此連坐受罰。悔恨懊惱之際遂有此問。

　　「怪人」的憤恨裡回響著亞當對上帝的提問：非自願地有了生命，此一生命了無趣味，卻如萬劫不復的懲罰，該要絕望自盡？或是要苟活下去，認命受苦，盼望那最終可能來到的救贖？這是十九世紀持懷疑論者依然在問的問題，尤其科學逐漸興起，神本位的創世論遭到日益強大的反思與挑戰。《科學怪人》的作者譴責了維克多，描寫了「怪人」驚悚的外貌與復仇行徑，但是她提出了一個基督教史上懸而未決的疑問：人類嘗試知識的禁果，探索科學，與基督教教義之間如何取得平衡？這是當時的巨大課題，今天的人類已習慣於高端科技帶來的便利和成就感。但是，試想一想，試管嬰兒、複製羊（人）等科技的發展，人類早已踩進了基督教教義主張的上帝的專權領土。這本小說寫作當時定義的「驚悚」，今天已成家常。人本思想強勢霸位，持續發燒，但人類感到幸福快樂了嗎？或是他／她們還在問與亞當同樣的問題？

Chapter 7 *Oliver Twist*

關於作者

查爾斯・狄更斯 (Charles Dickens, 1812–1870)
出生於英國樸次茅斯 (Portsmouth)，家中八個小孩，
他排行第二。父親擔任海軍職員，在他 12 歲時調
遷倫敦。狄更斯幼年由母親啟蒙，英文教育紮實，
也學習拉丁文，稍長進入正規小學，成績優異。狄
更斯的祖母擅長說故事，他小時耳濡目染，頗得真
傳，後來寫起小說，手法嫻熟，內容則帶自傳色彩，
再以觀察想像力渲染擴大，終成一代大師。

狄更斯剛出社會時擔任新聞記者，用「Boz」
這個筆名寫新聞稿，集結成為《博茲札記》(*Sketches
by Boz*)，暴露英國社會的黑暗面，吸引大量讀者關
注這些社會現狀。另外，他也用完全不同的詼諧筆調，出版了一冊小品文集《匹克威
克外傳》(*The Pickwick Papers*)，呈現他描寫人物的寫作才華。1837–1839 年，他出
版《孤雛淚》(*Oliver Twist*)，更展現他製造懸疑、抽絲剝繭的編故事文采。狄更斯了
解人性的善惡與喜好，因此能夠抓住讀者大眾的閱讀心理。《孤雛淚》的故事有親情
和愛情；有惡人和小人；還有錯綜複雜的鬥狠和鬥智，尤其描寫小人物的善良與無助，
處處都扣人心弦。這是狄更斯的第一部小說，也是他漫長寫作生涯的開端。

在往後的三十多年中，他再出版了十一本小說和其他文集，享譽歐美兩洲。
1841 年，他受邀到美國訪問，初時欣賞美國的立國精神，對新大陸的典章制度讚不
絕口，但發現自己作品遭到盜版，遂在波士頓公開演講中抨擊此事，與新聞界交惡，
剩餘的行程成了反高潮，十分不快。回國後，於 1842 年出版《美國紀行》(*American
Notes*)，揭發了新聞輿論的假民主，以及當時美國法治的不彰，尚未立法保障智慧財
產權，成為他對這個新世界的一大負評。

狄更斯探尋真相，嫉惡如仇，當新聞記者和小說家都不脫本色。他的作品充滿人
道關懷，故事情節高潮迭起，直至今日依然是一位舉世公認的大文豪。

查爾斯・狄更斯年表

1812

於樸次茅斯 (Portsmouth) 出生，父 John Dickens，母 Elizabeth Dickens

1836

《博茲札記》(*Sketches by Boz*) 出版、《匹克威克外傳》(*The Pickwick Papers*) 出版

1837-1839

《孤雛淚》(*Oliver Twist*) 出版、《尼古拉斯・尼克貝》(*Nicholas Nickleby*) 出版

1840

《老古玩店》(*The Old Curiosity Shop*) 出版

1841

《巴納比・拉奇》(*Barnaby Rudge*) 出版，隨後前往美國

1842

《美國紀行》(*American Notes*) 出版

1843

《小氣財神》(*A Christmas Carol*)、《馬丁・翟述偉》(*Martin Chuzzlewit*) 出版

1844-1846

周遊歐陸各國

1846-1848

《董貝父子》(*Dombey and Son*) 出版

1849

《塊肉餘生錄》(*David Copperfield*) 出版

1850

創辦刊物《家常話》(*Household Words*)

1852-1853

《荒涼山莊》(*Bleak House*) 出版

1854

《艱難時世》(*Hard Times*) 出版

1855-1857

《小杜麗》(*Little Dorrit*) 出版

1859

《雙城記》(*A Tale of Two Cities*) 出版、創辦刊物《一年四季》(*All the Year Round*)

1860-1861

《遠大前程》(*Great Expectations*) 出版

1870

因腦溢血逝世

One night, a pregnant woman was found lying on the street of an English town. No one knew where she had come from, so she was taken to the local workhouse*. After struggling to give birth to a baby boy, the exhausted woman pleaded, "Let me see the child, and die." When the baby was brought to her, she kissed his forehead and died.

The baby was given the name Oliver Twist by Mr. Bumble, the parish official, and sent to the nearby workhouse for orphans. There he spent a miserable childhood, badly treated and underfed*.

When he was nine, Oliver began to work in the workhouse. He was assigned to help with oakum* picking, that is, the untwisting of **strands**[1] from old rope. The boys did not receive adequate food for this hard labor, so many starved. One evening, they chose Oliver to request for more food. He asked the workhouse master, "Please, sir, I want some more."

The master became angry and called Mr. Bumble. Oliver was beaten and locked in a room. The parish officials offered a reward of five pounds to anyone who would take the troublesome boy. Mr. Sowerberry, the parish **coffin**[2]-maker, accepted the offer because he needed an assistant.

For Oliver, this was merely a move to a new scene of suffering. He had to sleep among the coffins and was fed the scraps* of meat prepared for the dog. Oliver was **bullied**[3] by the other assistant, an older boy named Noah Claypole. He and the servant Charlotte **mocked**[4] Oliver. Nevertheless, Mr. Sowerberry liked Oliver and made him his **apprentice**[5].

This made Noah jealous and he continued to **taunt**[6] Oliver. One day he cruelly insulted Oliver's dead mother. Oliver hit Noah and knocked him to the ground. Charlotte and Mrs. Sowerberry assisted Noah, and they all beat Oliver. Noah ran to get Mr. Bumble, accusing Oliver of trying to murder him and Charlotte. Consequently, Oliver was beaten again by Mr. Bumble.

Oliver knew life at the coffin-maker's would now be intolerable. Therefore, at dawn the next day he gathered some clothes and ran away.

He decided to walk to London, believing Mr. Bumble would never find him in that vast city. Oliver survived by begging. On the seventh day, he arrived in the town of Barnet. There he was greeted by a confident boy who introduced himself as Jack Dawkins, better known as the Artful Dodger. He bought Oliver food and took him to London. He promised Oliver that he would be given a place to live by his acquaintance, a respectable "old gentleman."

單字朗讀 完整 MP3 Ch7 Vocabulary

The Dodger led Oliver to an abandoned house in a poor part of the city. In an extremely dirty upstairs room Oliver met Fagin, an evil-looking old Jew with long **tangled**[7] red hair and a beard. A group of boys were there, smoking pipes and drinking spirits. A large number of silk handkerchiefs were hanging around the room.

Oliver did not realize that the boys had stolen the handkerchiefs for Fagin to sell. Two young women, Nancy and Bet, visited. They also assisted Fagin, but Oliver was too innocent to understand they were prostitutes*. Fagin began to train Oliver to take handkerchiefs from his pocket. Oliver thought it was a game.

Something You Should Know

英國社會嚴密的階級制度與貧富不均的問題，到了十九世紀後期，由於資本主義的弊端，窮人陷入前所未有的困境，圍繞貧民窟、虐待童工和管理不當的孤兒院衍生的日益嚴重的問題，終於逼使英國政府修定自十七世紀既有的《濟貧法》(*Poor Laws*) 使其更為周延。但是，徒法不足以自行，法條施行的細節，以及人為的蓄意不當操作，都會抵消濟貧的實效。《孤雛淚》曝露的就是有法但無實際作為的現實。

Words for Production

1. strand [strænd] *n.* [C]
   （線、繩等的）縷，股
2. coffin [`kɔfɪn] *n.* [C] 棺材；靈柩
3. bully [`bʊlɪ] *v.* 欺負；脅迫；傷害
4. mock [mɑk] *v.* 嘲笑，嘲弄
5. apprentice [ə`prɛntɪs] *n.* [C] 學徒
6. taunt [tɔnt] *v.* 譏諷；辱罵
7. tangled [`tæŋgl̩d] *adj.* 纏結的

Words for Recognition

* workhouse [`wɝk͵haʊs] *n.* [C]
  （英國舊時的）勞動濟貧所
* underfeed [͵ʌndɚ`fid] *v.* 未餵飽
* oakum [`okəm] *n.* [U]
  麻刀，麻絮（舊時由囚犯製造）
* scrap [skræp] *n.* (*usu. pl.*) 廚餘
* prostitute [`prɑstə͵tjut] *n.* [C] 妓女

Idioms and Phrases

1. give birth to sb 生孩子
2. assign sb to sth 指派⋯做⋯
3. known as sth 被稱作⋯的

Discussion

How serious was poverty a social problem during the Victorian era? Can you search online to find out related information? Share your findings with your class or friends.

One day, Fagin sent Oliver out with the Dodger and another boy, Charley Bates. They stopped behind an old gentleman reading a book at a bookstall*. The Dodger took a handkerchief from the gentleman's pocket. The two boys ran away, but Oliver was too slow. When the gentleman saw Oliver, he shouted "Stop thief!" A crowd chased Oliver and he was arrested.

At the police station the gentleman, Mr. Brownlow, felt sorry for the homeless* boy. Then the bookseller arrived and said another boy had stolen the handkerchief. When he left the building, Mr. Brownlow saw Oliver lying sick on the pavement*. He ordered a carriage and took him back to his house. There, Oliver was looked after and treated with **kindness**[8] for the first time in his young life.

Meanwhile, the Dodger and Charley Bates returned to Fagin. The old thief was furious that the police knew about the robbery. He feared Oliver would tell them his **whereabouts**[9]. Fagin decided to move to another house with his gang.

Then, Fagin arranged for Oliver to be **kidnapped**[10]. While Oliver was out on an errand for Mr. Brownlow, Nancy and her lover, the violent burglar Bill Sikes seized him and took him back to Fagin. Nevertheless, Nancy pitied Oliver and prevented Sikes and Fagin from beating him. Fagin threatened Oliver, making him be too afraid to try to escape.

Fagin persuaded Sikes to have Oliver assist him in robbing a country house. Sikes and two other robbers used Oliver to crawl through a small window to unlock the front door. However, they were heard by the servants who fired pistols. Oliver was wounded in the arm. Sikes dragged him away and they escaped. Because Oliver was too badly hurt to run, Sikes left him in a ditch.

Back in London, Fagin heard of the failed robbery. He secretly met a man called Monks in a pub to tell him the news. Monks had been looking for Oliver. He had been paying Fagin to make sure Oliver had a criminal record, though he did not tell Fagin why.

After Sikes left, Oliver lay unconscious. He woke up and **stumbled**[11] back towards the house for help. The servants recognized him as one of the thieves. However, Mrs.

Maylie, the old lady who owned the house, had **compassion**[12] for the child and summoned the family doctor. Mrs. Maylie and Miss Rose, a beautiful young woman whom she had adopted, took care of Oliver.

Oliver told them his history. As a result, the Maylies took him to London to look for Mr. Brownlow. They found that he had left London for the West Indies. They then took Oliver back with them to live happily in a cottage in a country village.

In London, Fagin discovered where Sikes was hiding and visited him. Nancy was looking after Sikes. Meanwhile, Monks arrived. The old thief took him to a private room. Nancy listened at the door. She overheard them talking about Oliver and realized his life was in danger.

Something You Should Know

　　「旅程」是小說中常見的敘事方法，藉此帶動情節的發展。奧立佛離開家鄉到了大都會倫敦，被一批黑幫歹徒控制，步步驚險，但最後終能化險為夷，認祖歸宗。這個敘事方法也見於《西遊記》、《綠野仙踪》(*Wizard of Oz*) 和《頑童歷險記》(*The Adventure of Huckleberry Finn*) 等小說中。主角們離家踏上險途，歷經磨練，終能成就自我。

Words for Production

8. kindness [ˋkaɪndnɪs] *n.* [U]
   仁慈；好意；體貼
9. whereabouts [͵hwɛrəˋbauts] *n.* [U]
   （某人或某物的）行蹤，下落，去向
10. kidnap [ˋkɪdnæp] *v.* 綁架；劫持
11. stumble [ˋstʌmbl] *v.* 跌跌撞撞地走
12. compassion [kəmˋpæʃən] *n.* [U] 同情心，憐憫

Words for Recognition

* bookstall [ˋbuk͵stɔl] *n.* [C] 書攤；報攤
* homeless [homləs] *adj.* 無家可歸的
* pavement [ˋpevmənt] *n.* [C] 人行道

Idioms and Phrases

4. too . . . to V 太⋯以致於⋯

Discussion

Can you think of another novel in which a journey is used as a symbol of quest for self-fulfillment?

Nancy heard that the Maylies were visiting London. She wanted to save Oliver, and therefore she secretly went to their hotel. Miss Rose was there. Nancy told her that Monks was Oliver's half-brother*, and that he had wrongly inherited all of their father's money. She promised to be on London Bridge every Sunday night between eleven and twelve to tell the story to whoever Miss Rose needed as a **witness**[13] to Oliver's parentage.

Miss Rose learned that Mr. Brownlow had returned to London. She went to see him and explained all that had happened to Oliver. Mr. Brownlow told Miss Rose they must meet Nancy to find out where to locate Monks.

Nancy told them where to find him. However, she had been followed. Fagin had become suspicious and had someone spy on the meeting. Nancy refused Mr. Brownlow's offer of a safe living place, saying she still loved Sikes.

Fagin told Sikes that Nancy had **betrayed**[14] them although she had actually got Mr. Brownlow to promise only to **prosecute**[15] Monks. In a fury, Sikes beat Nancy to death. He fled and was pursued by the police.

Mr. Brownlow found Monks and threatened to **expose**[16] his crimes unless he told the truth about Oliver. It was revealed that Monks' parents had an unhappy marriage. Monks' real name was Edward Leeford. After separating from his wife, Monks' father, Edwin Leeford, then fell in love with Oliver's mother, Agnes Fleming.

However, he had to leave on business and she was pregnant before he could marry her. He had left a will saying that his unborn child should have a share of his inheritance if the child did not become a criminal. He then suddenly fell ill and died. This is why Monks wanted Oliver to get a criminal record.

Monks told Mr. Brownlow that Agnes had run away because she had shamed her family by being pregnant outside marriage. She had traveled to be near the **grave**[17] of her baby's father. Her own father then also died, leaving her sister Rose in poverty. Mrs. Maylie, who lived nearby, had taken pity on Agnes' sister and raised her.

Finally, Monks agreed to sign a legal **document**[18] allowing Oliver to receive his share of the inheritance. Sikes was located by the police in an abandoned house. He accidently hung himself while using a rope to jump off a building. Fagin was arrested and sentenced to death. His gang members were imprisoned or transported to Australia. Monks left the country and died a few years later in an American prison.

Mr. Brownlow adopted Oliver as his son. He bought a house in the countryside near the Maylies and thus Oliver could live peacefully at last.

Something You Should Know

　　十九世紀中期到二十世紀初期的英國由女王維多利亞統治，稱為維多利亞時期 (Victorian Era)。維多利亞女王雖貴為一國之君，卻是一位賢妻良母，謹守禮教，並以此價值觀統攝社會風氣，嚴格界定女性的角色為相夫教子，沒有個人主體性，使得這段時期被史學家視為英國女權的黑暗年代。奧立佛的母親安妮‧弗萊明 (Agnes Fleming) 未婚生子，被認為恥辱之最，也使得奧立佛自小飽受欺凌。這就是為何狄更斯要為他洗白，解釋他父母當初原有婚約。

Words for Production

13. witness [`wɪtnɪs] *n.* [C] 目擊者
14. betray [bɪ`tre] *v.* 背叛，出賣
15. prosecute [`prɑsɪ͵kjut] *v.* 起訴；檢舉
16. expose [ɪk`spoz] *v.* 揭露，揭發
17. grave [grev] *n.* [C] 墳墓，墓穴
18. document [`dɑkjəmənt] *n.* [C]（尤指正式的）文件，公文

Words for Recognition

* half-brother [`hæf`brʌðɚ] *n.* [C] 同父異母（或同母異父）的兄弟
* parentage [`pɛrəntɪdʒ] *n.* [U] 出身，世系，家世

Idioms and Phrases

5. beat sb to death 打死…
6. fall in love with sb
   愛上…，與…相愛

Discussion

Can you find out more about the Victorian English society and its gender ethics? Discuss your findings in class or with friends.

一、閱讀測驗 (Reading Comprehension)

1. What's this story mainly about?

   (A) Oliver Twist and some of his best friends.

   (B) How Oliver Twist finally found his father.

   (C) Oliver Twist's miserable early years of life.

   (D) Why an old gentleman adopted Oliver Twist.

2. Which statements about the ends of characters in this story is **NOT** true?

   (A) Nancy was beaten to death by Sikes.

   (B) Fagin was murdered by Jack Dawkins.

   (C) Monks expired in an American prison.

   (D) Oliver lived peacefully with Mr. Brownlow.

3. Why did Monks want Oliver to have a criminal record?

   (A) To keep Oliver from getting a share of his father's wealth.

   (B) To throw Oliver into jail and make his life more miserable.

   (C) To take revenge on Oliver for stealing many handkerchiefs.

   (D) To make Oliver a criminal and expel him to other countries.

4. What can we infer from this story?

   (A) More orphanages should be built to shelter more poor orphans.

   (B) Oliver was blessed because many people were willing to help him.

   (C) Young children like Oliver were vulnerable and prone to be fooled.

   (D) In the society where Oliver lived, human rights were almost ignored.

二、字彙填充 (Fill in the Blanks)

_____ 1. It's courageous to e_____ed this scandal to the public.

_____ 2. Ms. Lee tried her best to stop Hanks from b_____ying other classmates.

_____ 3. Maggie had c_____n for the old beggar and gave him a fair amount of money.

三、引導式翻譯 (Guided Translation)

1. 當 Richard 第一次遇到 Christine 時就愛上她了。

   Richard _____ _____ _____ _____ Christine when he met her for the first time.

2. Sam 的太太昨晚順利生下一名健康的嬰兒。

   Sam's wife smoothly _____ _____ _____ a healthy baby last night.

3. 那個女孩太害怕而無法自己一個人走進那個黑暗的房間。

   The girl was _____ afraid _____ walk into the dark room by herself.

賞析

　　《孤雛淚》是狄更斯的第一部小說，之前他擅長報導社會黑暗角落的不公不義事件，用銳利的文筆為弱勢發聲。《孤雛淚》的故事主軸為奧立佛的貧寒出身，成長的過程被一隻幕後黑手蒙克斯（同父異母的哥哥）操縱，為了圖謀他分內的遺產，用盡心計引誘他走上歧途。幸虧奧立佛本性善良，加上貴人相助，因此最終苦盡甘來，找到自己的親人，也順利繼承了遺產。

　　狄更斯伸張社會正義，暴露了當時社會最為人詬病的兩大弊害：壓榨童工和不人道的孤兒院管理制度。狄更斯對英國的窮人深感同情。按照當時英國的法律，欠債的人要被關進監獄裡。他在 12 歲時，父母因不善理財，遭債主舉報索債，因而入獄，後來幸好有祖母過世留下的錢，才得以保釋出獄。父母入獄後，狄更斯被送去一家血汗工廠當學徒童工，為鞋油罐子黏貼標籤，工作過勞、食不飽腹，又常遭打罵。這段苦澀的童年經驗在他的小說裡化為不同的情節，呈現出他對悲涼生活的切身感受，也深深體會窮人在英國社會結構下薄弱的人權。

　　《孤雛淚》中一段經典情節帶有自傳色彩：「奧立佛在孤兒院中向院方乞求多一口食物，而遭責罰。」這是當時社會底層階級的每日經驗，尤其兒童勞工被剝奪正常的童年和心智成長，更是對人權的極端摧殘。資本階級將童工美其名稱為「學徒」(apprentice)，其實對待他們如同奴工。

　　大都會如倫敦的另一個怪象便是盜賊橫行，甚至形成黑幫黨派，巧取豪奪、以大欺小、以惡欺善。小說中的人物善惡分明，惡人如費金和賽克斯，對比於奧立佛和南西，力量過於懸殊，小說情節曲折起伏，讀者在閱讀過程中，心理上深深地認同弱勢的好人，既同情又為他們擔憂。當年這本小說每月出刊一次，引得萬千讀者懸念等候，大為轟動。

　　狄更斯深知世風敗壞，無權勢的好人是社會的邊緣人，但是《孤雛淚》的結局卻是光明正義的，奧立佛盼到了親情和財富，不再需要過著擔憂、煩惱的生活，實現了「好人有好報」的理念。狄更斯這一安排可以說是伸張「詩的公義」（poetic justice，指文學作品當中善有善報，惡有惡報的故事結局），用以抗衡真實社會弱肉強食的叢林法則 (jungle law)。作者藉此也抒發了自身的人權價值信念。

Chapter 8 *Jane Eyre*

關於作者

夏綠蒂‧勃朗特 (Charlotte Brontë, 1816–1855) 出生於英國約克郡，家中排行第三，也是勃朗特三姊妹中年紀最大的。5歲喪母後，夏綠蒂與四名姊妹和一名弟弟離家依靠阿姨生活。之後，四個姊妹被送到當地一所教會開辦的寄宿學校，期間姊妹中兩人（瑪麗亞、伊麗莎白）感染肺結核病故，剩下夏綠蒂和愛蜜莉 (Emily) 旋即輟學回家。數年之後，夏綠蒂繼續求學，成為教師，但選擇離開正式教職，去當家庭女教師 (governess)，寄宿富有的僱主家，教導他們家中未成年的女兒。

夏綠蒂曾想自已辦校，但未成功，後來專職寫作，與愛蜜莉成為英國文學史上知名的小說家。兩人和另一妹妹安妮 (Anne) 利用男性名字 (Currer Bell、Ellis Bell、Acton Bell) 作為筆名，開始出版詩集，但乏人問津，三人轉而寫作小說。1847 年，夏綠蒂的第一本小說《教師》(*The Professor*) 的書稿找不到出版商願意出書，直到 1857 年才出版。1847 年底，《簡愛》(*Jane Eyre*) 出版，為她贏得遲來的名聲。有生之年，她又出版了《雪莉》(*Shirley*) 和《維萊特》(*Villette*) 兩本小說。

夏綠蒂・勃朗特年表

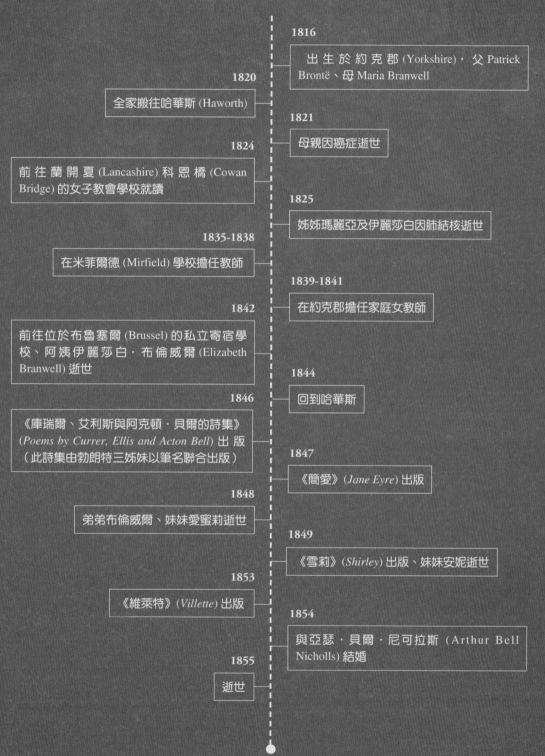

1816
出生於約克郡 (Yorkshire)，父 Patrick Brontë、母 Maria Branwell

1820
全家搬往哈華斯 (Haworth)

1821
母親因癌症逝世

1824
前往蘭開夏 (Lancashire) 科恩橋 (Cowan Bridge) 的女子教會學校就讀

1825
姊姊瑪麗亞及伊麗莎白因肺結核逝世

1835-1838
在米菲爾德 (Mirfield) 學校擔任教師

1839-1841
在約克郡擔任家庭女教師

1842
前往位於布魯塞爾 (Brussel) 的私立寄宿學校、阿姨伊麗莎白・布倫威爾 (Elizabeth Branwell) 逝世

1844
回到哈華斯

1846
《庫瑞爾、艾利斯與阿克頓・貝爾的詩集》(*Poems by Currer, Ellis and Acton Bell*) 出版（此詩集由勃朗特三姊妹以筆名聯合出版）

1847
《簡愛》(*Jane Eyre*) 出版

1848
弟弟布倫威爾、妹妹愛蜜莉逝世

1849
《雪莉》(*Shirley*) 出版、妹妹安妮逝世

1853
《維萊特》(*Villette*) 出版

1854
與亞瑟・貝爾・尼可拉斯 (Arthur Bell Nicholls) 結婚

1855
逝世

As a young orphan, Jane Eyre was sent to live with her wealthy aunt, Sarah Reed. The woman had three children of her own, two girls and a boy, who were Jane's cousins. Sarah Reed showered her three children with affection but was cruel and unloving to Jane. Of the three cousins, the boy, John, bullied Jane often.

One day, John fought with Jane over a book. When the boy threw the book at Jane, it hit her and she fell, knocking her head against a door and drawing blood. "Wicked and cruel boy!" Jane yelled, and the boy came at her. Having been hit many times by the boy, Jane fought back **viciously**[1], and the boy screamed in pain and yelled, "Rat! Rat!"

When Sarah Reed came to the scene of the fight, she had Jane taken to the room in the house known as the red-room. It was a room Jane feared, for it was where Mr. Reed had died. Filled with fear and **superstition**[2], Jane thought she had seen her uncle's ghost and lost consciousness.

After being treated for her condition, Jane learned she would be sent to the Lowood School. On the day she left her aunt's estate early in the morning, no one in her extended family* got up to bid her good-bye.

Jane found the Lowood School to be a difficult place to get along. The teachers were strict, and the headmaster was very **stingy**[3]. The girls at the school were hungry and cold for much of the time, but Jane found a friend named Helen Burns. A typhus epidemic* hit, and many students became sick and died. Her friend Helen was also sick, but with **tuberculosis**[4]. Jane went to Helen's room to be with her, and Helen died while the two girls were sleeping.

Something You Should Know

家庭女教師 (governess) 在十九世紀的英國社會是一個很特殊的職業，由未婚女性住宿於貴族或富人家中，教導未成年孩童的功課，包括英文讀寫和算術，一直到他們成長邁入下一個人生階段。這些女性來自中產階級家庭，受過良好教育，但因經濟壓力，必需出外自謀生計。在僱主家中她們的地位尷尬，不是僕人，也不算家人，要遵守主人家規，平時毫無個人的社交生活，因此也不可能期盼有正常的婚姻機會。這樣子的女性社群是一個時代的矛盾體，既能憑才學養活自己，但同時又受到父權社會的制約，不能成為自主的個體。故事中的簡是個成功突破社會障礙的這類女性，這本小說可以視為對她的禮讚。作者在虛構的故事中伸張了那個年代被壓抑的女權。

單字朗讀 完整 MP3 Ch8 Vocabulary

Jane ended up spending eight years at Lowood School. She was a student for six, and in the last two years, a teacher. However, Jane longed to go out in the world and experience more, so she placed an advertisement to be a tutor for a child. Her advertisement was answered, and Jane took a position as governess* at Thornfield, a manor about 50 miles from Lowood School.

Arriving at Thornfield, Jane met the child she would teach, a young French girl named Adele. She also met the master of the manor*, Mr. Rochester, and began to fall in love with him. Jane enjoyed working with the child, but she wondered about the mysterious screams and noises she occasionally heard. One night, Jane was woken by a horrible laugh, and went to investigate. She found Mr. Rochester's room in flames, but she couldn't wake him. She extinguished* the fire and saved his life.

Some time later, Jane was walking in the orchard at Thornfield, and Mr. Rochester called her over. He professed* his love for her and asked her to marry him. Extremely surprised and in disbelief, Jane accepted his proposal.

Words for Production

1. viciously [ˋvɪʃəslɪ] *adv.* 激烈地
2. superstition [ˌsupɚˋstɪʃən] *n.* [C][U] 迷信
3. stingy [ˋstɪdʒɪ] *adj.* 小氣的，吝嗇的
4. tuberculosis [tjuˌbɚkjəˋlosɪs] *n.* [U] 肺結核

Words for Recognition

* extended family [ɪkˋstɛndɪd ˋfæmlɪ] *n.* [C]（幾代同堂的）大家庭
* typhus epidemic [ˋtaɪfəs ˌɛpəˋdɛmɪk] *n.* [C] 斑疹傷寒（由蝨子傳播）流行病
* governess [ˋgʌvɚnɪs] *n.* [C]（尤指舊時的）家庭女教師
* manor [ˋmænɚ] *n.* [C] 莊園宅第
* extinguish [ɪkˋstɪŋgwɪʃ] *v.* 熄滅
* profess [prəˋfɛs] *v.* 聲稱；自稱；謊稱

Idioms and Phrases

1. shower sb with sth 大量給予…（禮物或讚美）
2. long to do sth 渴望…

Discussion

Ghosts and other supernatural elements often are found in Gothic novels. In this part, and later in the novel, do you think these elements are used persuasively? Do they make the novel more compelling?

課文朗讀 分段 MP3 Track 8-2

Preparations were made for Mr. Rochester and Jane's wedding. One night, a wild woman came into Jane's room and tore her bridal* veil in two. She told the story to Mr. Rochester, who had her sleep in a different room in the manor on the night before the wedding.

Just as Mr. Rochester and Jane were exchanging **vows**[5] at the church, a voice called out that the wedding could not happen. The voice belonged to Mr. Mason, who stated that Mr. Rochester was already married. As a young man, Rochester had married a woman in Jamaica*, and that woman had gone mad. It turned out that this mad woman, Bertha, was kept hidden on the third floor of the manor. It was Bertha's screams that Jane had heard, and it was also Bertha who had started the fire in Mr. Rochester's room and tore Jane's bridal veil in half.

Learning all of this information depressed Jane greatly. Mr. Rochester wanted her to run away to France with him, and the decision she had to make tore her apart. She finally decided that she could not become Mr. Rochester's **mistress**[6]. Taking a little money and a few possessions she had, Jane **fled**[7] Thornfield in the middle of the night.

Jane took a coach as far as her money would take her. Getting out of the coach, she accidentally left the rest of her meager* belongings inside it. Now penniless*, Jane was forced to sleep outdoors for the night. The next day, she came to a town. At a bakery, she tried to exchange a handkerchief or her gloves for something to eat. The woman in the store refused her, and Jane walked on. At a farmhouse, she found a farmer eating brown bread and cheese. Jane begged him for food, and he cut her a thick slice of bread.

Jane traveled on and finally came to a house where there were two ladies, a gentleman and a servant woman. When she knocked on the door, the servant told her to go away and closed the door. Jane **collapsed**[8] on the ground, and at that point she heard a voice. It was Mr. St. John Rivers, and he let her come into his house. He had been listening to the servant and Jane's talk.

Something You Should Know

「出走」(departure) 是小說家愛用的敘事方法，尤其在成長小說如《簡愛》中，主角遇到挫折不願喪志，反而鼓起勇氣離家奮鬥，期待轉機。古典文學中有一類故事稱為「英雄神話」(hero myth)，講述英雄人物的成長過程，歷經「離家→淬煉→成功→返家」的階段，最後得以繼承家業光大門楣。簡可以說是女性版的英雄。

Words for Production

5. vow [vaʊ] *n.* [C] 誓言；誓約
6. mistress [`mɪstrɪs] *n.* [C] 情婦
7. flee [fli] *v.* （尤指因危險或恐懼而）逃跑
8. collapse [kə`læps] *v.* （因疾病或虛弱而）倒下，昏倒
9. split [splɪt] *v.* 使分開；使裂開
10. missionary [`mɪʃənˌɛrɪ] *n.* [C] 傳教士
11. harshly [harʃlɪ] *adv.* 嚴酷的

Words for Recognition

* bridal [`braɪdl] *adj.* 新娘的；婚禮的
* Jamaica [dʒə`mekə] *n.* 牙買加
* meager [`migɚ] *adj.* （數量）很少的，不足的
* penniless [`pɛnlɪs] *adj.* 身無分文的
* evenly [`ivənlɪ] *adv.* 平均地；相等地
* newfound [njuˈfaʊnd] *adj.* 新獲得的；新發現的

Idioms and Phrases

3. belong to sb 屬於…，歸…所有
4. tear sb apart 使…極其難受
5. put sth off 延後…，拖延…

Jane lived with the Rivers for a time, and eventually she learned that she was related to them, they were her cousins. Jane also learned that her uncle had died and left her a large inheritance. Out of gratitude, Jane decided to evenly* **split**[9] the inheritance with her newfound* family.

St. John Rivers decided to become a **missionary**[10] and travel to India. However, he wanted Jane to come with him and become his wife. Jane still loved Mr. Rochester very much and told St. John that they did not love each other as a husband and wife should.

St. John Rivers kept pursuing Jane, and he put off his trip to India. He told Jane that if she didn't obey him, she was going against God. Then he acted **harshly**[11] toward her, and this caused Jane to hate him.

Discussion

Do you think Jane is right to flee Thornfield under the circumstances? Would that be a cruel decision for Mr. Rochester?

Before dinner one evening, St. John Rivers said a prayer, and the words moved Jane. She knew he had a lot of talents as a speaker, and she began to doubt herself. She wondered if she should give in, marry St. John, and move to India with him. Right at that moment, she had a strange feeling in her body. Her heart started beating fast, and St. John asked her what was wrong. At that moment, Jane heard Mr. Rochester's voice saying, "Jane! Jane! Jane!"

The next day, Jane took a coach back to Thornfield. Arriving, she had to walk two miles to the manor from the coach stop. Jane found the whole manor was in **ruins**[12], with windows broken and the roof caved in. The stones were blackened*, showing **evidence**[13] of a terrible fire. No one was there, so Jane left and went back to the town to find out what happened.

At an inn called the Rochester Arms, Jane questioned a man about Thornfield. He told her that the woman Bertha had started the fire. Mr. Rochester had saved the servants, and also tried to save Bertha, who had run up to the roof. Mr. Rochester had called to Bertha, but she jumped and ended her life. Although Mr. Rochester survived the fire, he lost one of his hands and also his sight. The man at the inn then told Jane where Mr. Rochester was—at a manor house called Ferndean, found in a desolate* spot about 30 miles away.

Jane traveled to Ferndean immediately. It was buried deep in the woods, and was a very old manor house. Mr. Rochester lived there with two of his servants, John and Mary. When Jane arrived, it was night, and she saw Mr. Rochester inside. She thought that he looked much the same as he used to, but had a sad, lonely look on his face.

Jane knocked on the door, and Mary answered it. She was very surprised to see Jane at such a late hour, and the servant was just about to bring Mr. Rochester a tray with candles and water. Jane took the tray from the servant and brought it in to Mr. Rochester instead. When she entered the room, Mr. Rochester's dog, Pilot, heard Jane, and **bounded**[14] towards her happily, almost causing Jane to drop the tray. When she

---

Something You Should Know

　　小說的結尾男女主角相愛相惜，組成美滿家庭，實現性別平等的理想，消弭了最初兩人在社會階級和經濟能力上的差距，一消一長產生和諧，反映英國傳統社會的文化潛規則。在今日看來，這樣的性別平等仍有侷限（簡嫁的是落魄眼盲之後的羅徹斯特），但是在當時的文化之下，這樣的結局安排已然深具顛覆力，更能顯現女性的韌性。

told the dog to lie down, Mr. Rochester heard her voice and thought he might be dreaming. Learning this was not the case, he **wrapped**[15] his arms around Jane.

Mr. Rochester gave thanks to God that Jane had come back to him. He and Jane patched up their relationship and married in a small, quiet church. As the story ended, Jane told of being married for 10 wonderful years. Mr. Rochester, after two years of **blindness**[16], also began to regain his vision. He could see out of one eye, and he was able to see their first son at his birth.

Words for Production

12. ruin [`ruɪn] *n.* [C] 廢墟；殘垣斷壁
13. evidence [`ɛvədəns] *n.* [U] 證據
14. bound [baʊnd] *v.* 跳動；跳躍著前進
15. wrap [ræp] *v.* 用…纏繞
16. blindness [`blaɪndnɪs] *n.* [U] 盲，失明

Words for Recognition

* blacken [`blækən] *v.* 使…變成黑色
* desolate [`dɛslɪt] *adj.* 荒涼的

Idioms and Phrases

6. give in 妥協，（先是拒絕，後來）勉強同意，讓步
7. cave in 塌陷；坍塌
8. patch sth up 彌補…（關係）

Discussion

What are the admirable traits you find in Jane that enable her to succeed in the end?

一、閱讀測驗 (Reading Comprehension)

1. Which of the following statements about this story is **NOT** true?

   (A) One of Jane's cousins, John, often bullied her.

   (B) Jane's friend Helen went to Thornfield with her.

   (C) When Jane's uncle died, he left her a large inheritance.

   (D) Jane finally married Mr. Rochester in a small, quiet church.

2. Why did Jane Eyre turn down St. John Rivers when he proposed to her?

   (A) Because she didn't want to go to India with him.

   (B) Because she thought he was not wealthy enough.

   (C) Because she still loved Mr. Rochester very deeply.

   (D) Because St. John Rivers had already got married.

3. What happened to Mr. Rochester after Jane Eyre left Thornfield?

   (A) Some bandits broke into his manor and took away everything.

   (B) He was so heartbroken as to kill Bertha and commit suicide.

   (C) He went broke and then became a beggar wandering around.

   (D) His manor was burned down and he was seriously wounded.

4. What can we infer about Jane Eyre's personality?

   (A) She was a strong woman who wouldn't surrender to fate easily.

   (B) She was a romantic woman who dreamed of a happy marriage.

   (C) She was a vulnerable woman who needed others to protect her.

   (D) She was a pessimistic woman who often complained about her fate.

二、字彙填充 (Fill in the Blanks)

_____ 1. You are supposed to present solid e_____e to prove your new theory.

_____ 2. Although Mr. Wang is very rich, he is quite s_____y to others.

_____ 3. After finishing the marathon, the runner suddenly c_____ed due to exhaustion.

三、引導式翻譯 (Guided Translation)

1. Rita 熱愛唱歌，而且渴望成為知名的流行歌手。

   Rita is passionate about singing and _____ _____ _____ a famous popular singer.

2. 在這個房間裡的所有古董都屬於 Gary 的祖父。

   All the antiques in this room _____ _____ Gary's grandfather.

3. 由於有一個強烈颱風正在接近當中，我們別無選擇，只能延後日本之旅。

   With a strong typhoon approaching, we have no choice but to _____ _____ our trip to Japan.

賞析

　　《簡愛》常被稱為一部「哥德式的女性成長小說」(Gothic female Bildungsroman)，寫一名弱女子困於孤兒出身和性別的雙重障礙，棲身於富人家庭擔任家教，受盡顛沛流離之後終能自立，於是勇敢回頭追求真愛，覓得良緣，也成就自己堅強的人格。故事中摻入了超自然的情節，例如，寄居舅媽家的某日，簡動手反抗表弟，被舅媽懲罰禁閉於舅舅病逝的那間恐怖暗室 (red-room)。簡在極度恐懼之下，嘶吼尖叫說，見到舅舅的鬼魂，接著暈倒過去，舅媽因此同意讓她離家上學。另外，在故事後段，簡意外遇到親人，繼承了一筆遺產，但因思念羅徹斯特，又苦於表哥強勢求婚的壓力，心力交瘁而萌發屈服的念頭，此時耳邊忽然聽見羅徹斯特呼喊自己的名字，當下毅然下定決心，回頭尋找心所企盼的人。

　　這兩段「哥德式」的超自然情節對於女主角的人格成長具有重要的意義。前一段情節之後，舅媽同意把她送到羅伍德 (Lowood) 寄宿學校就讀。簡在這所學校經歷過度嚴格的管教，生活條件極差，校長假藉鍛鍊學生身心的藉口，苛扣學校經費中飽私囊，導致爆發傷寒。這件事引起公眾注意，校長去職，由新校長接任。簡度過這場災難，在學校讀了幾年，畢業後留下來教了兩年書。簡見到鬼魂暈倒，才有了離家受教育的機會。第二段情節更為關鍵，簡聽到心儀的人呼喊自己，終於放下猶豫，拋開身分地位的自卑，以及認為自己介入羅徹斯特婚姻的罪惡感，勇敢回頭。故事的背景為十九世紀中葉的英國社會，那時的社會依然呈現男尊女卑的狀態，並且中產階級女性受教育和工作的機會十分有限，小說的結局明顯具有顛覆傳統禮教的力道。

　　簡的成長過程與三個地方密切相關：羅伍德、桑菲爾德 (Thornfield) 和弗恩丁 (Ferndean)。羅伍德以殘酷的方式惕勵了她的體魄。在桑菲爾德，簡陷入主僕之間違反禮教的初戀，經歷失火和瘋女的不尋常事，婚禮之前又橫生變故。這種種的挫折卻沒能把她擊倒，離開桑菲爾德踏上流浪之路後又是另一番淬鍊，在走頭無路之時幸遇表親，更因為得到一筆遺產而成為經濟獨立的女子。至此，簡已經擺脫了她的孤貧的出身，能夠與羅徹斯特的社會地位相匹配了。她回到弗恩丁，與眼盲的羅徹斯特結婚，兩年之後羅徹斯特重見光明，能夠見到自己的兒子出生，故事有了圓滿的結局。此時的簡與羅徹斯特在經濟、社會地位和性別等方面都已經是平等的主體，她和他成為快樂的夫妻，也是心靈契合的伙伴。《簡愛》對於身心成長和性別平等有細膩的體現。

閱讀經典文學時光之旅：美國篇

陳彰範／編著

八篇故事、八篇有關勇氣、野心、迷失與療癒傷痕的美國經典文學

　　美國文學相較其他國家，崛起甚晚。早期作品多自歐洲文學的風格延伸而來，爾後也觸及社會狀況，描寫殖民時期的美國、戰爭的苦痛與慘烈、黑人於白人社會的掙扎等。文學刻劃出當代複雜情勢，勾勒出虛偽或善良的人性，反映人們奔放或壓抑的心理。本書選文涵蓋十八至二十世紀，空間廣納城市、鄉村及海洋。描述時代遞嬗之下，當代人民的希望與苦難──文學並不難懂，文學就是另一個時代的你和我。透過閱讀，你我得以跨越時空，一窺那已無法觸及的世界。

★ 精選美國經典文學作品，囊括各類議題，如性別平等、人權、海洋教育等。
★ 獨家收錄故事背景的知識補充及原文講解。
★ 附精闢賞析、文章中譯及電子朗讀音檔，自學也能輕鬆讀懂文學作品。
★ 可搭配 108 課綱英文多元選修、加深加廣課程。

活用英文：實用的英文閱讀訓練
Reading Comprehension of Real Life: A Training for Practical Skills

王信雲、李秋芸／編著
Ian Fletcher ／審定

★ 全書分為旅遊交通、生活、飲食、大眾傳播等四大單元，每單元含 15 回圖表閱讀測驗，共計 60 篇。生活化內容，作答同時可以熟悉生活中的英文。

★ 結合 PISA 圖表式閱讀測驗元素，除了選擇題外，更有開放式及封閉式問答題。並採取未來新課綱「卷卡合一」的作答模式，提前熟悉素養導向的新題型。

★ 可搭配 108 課綱加深加廣「英語閱讀與寫作」課程。

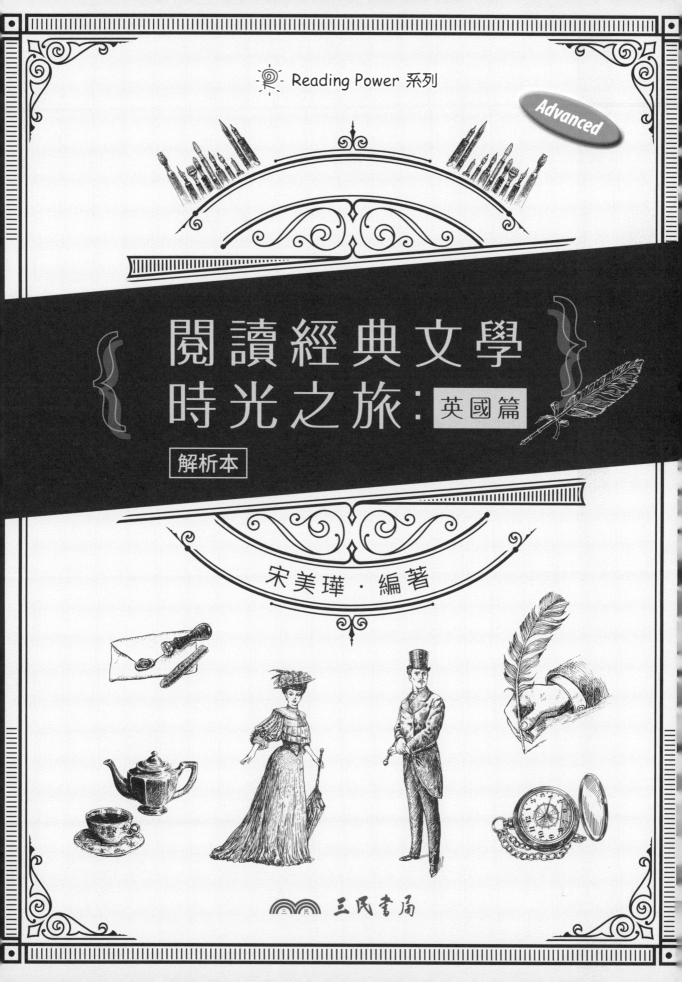

Reading Power 系列

Advanced

閱讀經典文學
時光之旅：英國篇

解析本

宋美瑾・編著

三民書局

Contents

貝奧武夫

　　貝奧武夫是一名戰士，聞名於日耳曼各族之間。他擁有皇室的血統，是基特族國王海格拉克的姪子。在這個時代的貴族奉行英雄主義。在他的行為舉止上，貝奧武夫是英雄生活方式的完美典範。他很勇敢，在戰場上叱吒風雲，對國王盡忠，並且以自己的功績為傲。

　　據說這個威猛的戰士擁有三十個人的力量。他在戰役中擊敗無數個進犯自己國家的敵人，藉此建立了自己的名聲。他最有名的事件就是與另外一個戰士（他的兒時好友布瑞卡）的游泳競賽傳奇。當時他們都很年輕，一起挑戰看誰能帶著劍跳入冰冷的海中，殺死海怪。他們在水中游泳戰鬥了五個晝夜。有一隻怪物想要把貝奧武夫拉進海底，但是他親手殺了這隻怪物和其他八隻，帶著勝利回到岸上。

　　當貝奧武夫聽說有一隻可怕的怪物攻擊了丹麥國王赫羅斯加的宮殿，他決心要去幫助這個王國。貝奧武夫雄心壯志，要打響自己的名號。此外，他跟丹麥國王也有深厚情誼。赫羅斯加曾經以贈送金銀財寶的方式，幫助貝奧武夫的父親終結一場與其他部族血淋淋的爭鬥。

　　就這樣，貝奧武夫與十四個他最信賴的戰士出航去丹麥。他們來到赫羅斯加所建立的大宮殿。在這所宮殿中，赫羅斯加建立了他的王權。這個宮殿過去代表了丹麥人的力量與名位，可是現在他成為了這個王國麻煩的焦點。在向赫羅斯加致意並進獻禮物之後，貝奧武夫詢問有關這隻怪物的訊息。

　　他得知這隻邪惡的怪物，叫做格倫戴爾，住在宮殿外圍的沼澤地與荒野中。格倫戴爾聽到戰士們在歡慶並讚頌神，就變得異常憤怒。有一個晚上，牠攻擊了在宮殿裡沉睡的戰士，把這三十個戰士抓回牠自己的沼澤巢穴，在那裡屠戮了他們，並以他們的血肉大快朵頤。這夜晚的突襲就這樣持續了十二年，很多戰士相繼遇害。武器沒辦法傷害這個怪物，因此丹麥人在晚上格倫戴爾出沒的時候，就必須放棄這座宮殿。

　　貝奧武夫宣稱他可以赤手空拳打敗這個可怕的強敵。他誇耀自己的功績，與殺死一眾海怪的壯舉。丹麥人受到他流利的演講所鼓舞，閃現的希望取代了他們的憂鬱。在那個晚上，貝奧武夫與十四個基特戰士待在宮殿裡，等待著。

　　突然，他們聽到門被拆毀的聲音。格倫戴爾闖了進來。這隻怪物吃掉了一個戰士，然後想要抓起貝奧武夫。然而，貝奧武夫抓住怪物的手，讓牠無法逃脫。被這強大的力量緊抓住，格倫戴爾嚇壞了。牠想要掙脫，他們就這樣在宮廷中扭打著。

最後，貝奧武夫折斷了格倫戴爾的整條手臂，結束了這場戰鬥。重傷的格倫戴爾蹣跚跟蹌地回到牠的沼澤地，一命嗚呼。

為了證明自己的勝利，貝奧武夫將格倫戴爾的手臂懸掛在宮殿的牆上。赫羅斯加跟他的戰士們看到這個戰利品，覺得喜出望外，接著將貝奧武夫歌頌為最強悍的英雄。

國王赫羅斯加特別舉辦了一個宴會為貝奧武夫慶功。在慶功宴上，他給了貝奧武夫金銀財寶、武器與盔甲。人們創作詩歌讚頌這個英雄。這是一個歡樂的慶祝。在經年累月的混亂與苦難之後，丹麥王國重建了秩序。在宴會過後的晚上，國王跟他的戰士們在宮殿中睡覺，他們相信自己終於不會再遇到災禍。

這些人完全沒有想到新的威脅出現了。格倫戴爾的母親是另外一隻野蠻的怪物。牠看到垂死的兒子，心中瞬間燃起熊熊怒火。牠下定決心，要向奪走牠兒子性命的這些人報仇雪恨。當丹麥人還在沉睡時，牠穿過荒野，闖進宮殿，抓住赫羅斯加的親信艾斯吉爾，殺害了他。然後牠偷走了掛在牆上的格倫戴爾的手臂。戰士群起攻擊牠，可是格倫戴爾的母親帶著受害者的屍體與兒子的殘肢，逃進了暗處。

赫羅斯加召喚貝奧武夫入宮，請求他再次幫助自己的子民。貝奧武夫同意了，並發誓說要找到格倫戴爾母親的巢穴，親手消滅牠。因此，貝奧武夫與他強大的基特戰士們進入了荒野。他們來到了一個險峻的懸崖邊，眺望一個湖，湖中水浪翻騰。在湖的深處升起濃郁的血水。他們驚駭地看到可怕的生物，像是巨大的水蛇，還有海中的大蛟龍，在這險惡的水域中出沒。艾斯吉爾的頭被平放在懸崖上，那時他們就知道自己已經來到格倫戴爾母親的巢穴。

貝奧武夫潛入湖中，直到湖的深處。他幾乎花了一天的時間才到達湖的底端。他在那裡被海中的怪物包圍。格倫戴爾的母親抓住他，把他拖進自己的住所。貝奧武夫的劍無法傷害牠，所以他用盡全力與這怪物扭打。他無法打倒怪物，眼看就要輸了這場戰鬥。在這時，這筋疲力盡的戰士看到了懸掛在牆上的一把巨大的劍，他抓住這把劍，砍向怪物的頸部。鮮血自傷口湧出，格倫戴爾的母親死了。貝奧武夫看到旁邊格倫戴爾的屍體，便砍下了屍體的頭，帶著這可怕的戰利品游回水面。

湖邊的戰士們看到水裡有鮮血湧現，他們以為這是貝奧武夫的血，感覺大事不妙。可是當他們的首領出現在湖面上，抓著格倫戴爾的頭，他們的絕望就被欣喜取代。這幫戰士帶著勝利的消息回到宮殿，丹麥人為他們歡呼，稱他們為英雄。赫羅斯加大大地獎賞了貝奧武夫，為這英雄與他的戰士們舉辦了另外一場慶功宴。丹麥人與基特人就這樣互相宣示忠誠與友誼，然後貝奧武夫就帶著他的戰士們啟航回到家鄉。

戰士歸國，在貝奧武夫的叔叔——基特族國王海格拉克——的宮殿裡面受到熱烈的歡迎。貝奧武夫在宮廷上訴說自己在丹麥的冒險事蹟，也提到他如何受到赫羅斯加國王殷勤的款待。他活靈活現地敘述了自己如何在宮殿中打敗格倫戴爾，以及在荒蕪

的湖底打敗了格倫戴爾的母親，從而拯救了丹麥人，得到了他們的讚揚。接著，貝奧武夫慷慨地把他從丹麥國王那邊得到的獎賞，大部分都獻給了海格拉克國王。海格拉克讚譽貝奧武夫是個真正的英雄，並且給予他封地與一些自己的財產。

幾年過後，海格拉克國王在與瑞典王國的戰爭中捐軀。貝奧武夫繼承了王位，打敗了基特族的敵人。他英明的統治持續了半個世紀，為國家帶來了和平與繁榮昌盛。然而，在這太平盛世將要結束的時候，基特王國必須面對一個與格倫戴爾母子同樣可怕的災禍。

幾個世紀之前，某個古老族群的生還者將財寶埋在一個古墳之中。一隻兇猛的龍發現了這分財寶，小心地在旁邊守護，持續了好幾百年。有一天，一個盜賊進入了這座古墓，在這野獸睡著的時候，偷走了一個鑲滿珠寶的杯子。這隻龍醒來之後，發現杯子不見了，從古墳中飛出來，追獵這個侵入者，所到之處烈火焚燒。這隻龍無法找到盜賊，勃然大怒，每天晚上都攻擊基特人民。這隻龍找到了國王貝奧武夫的宮殿，將它燒毀殆盡。

儘管這時的貝奧武夫已經非常老了，他還是覺得保衛基特人民，對抗這隻兇猛的生物，是自己的職責。他穿上自己的盔甲，帶著十一個最勇猛的戰士來到這隻龍所在的座古墳。貝奧武夫對龍提出挑戰，龍就開始攻擊貝奧武夫。可是國王年事已高，失去了大部分戰鬥的氣力。然而，他還是英勇地戰鬥，後來龍咬了貝奧武夫的頸部，造成他的重傷。

在那之後，貝奧武夫所有的同行戰士因恐懼竄逃，只有一個戰士，偉格列夫，堅守崗位，決心要跟隨國王與龍一決死戰。這位勇敢的戰士把劍刺入龍的腹部，給了貝奧武夫一個機會可以抽出刀子，刺向這頭野獸的側腹。這頭龍受到重傷，當場死亡。而貝奧武夫感到他脖子上的傷口開始抽痛並灼燒，他知道龍的噬咬帶有毒性。

瀕死的貝奧武夫要求偉格列夫照顧他的族人。偉格列夫感到很可恥，因為這些戰士們貪生怕死而沒有救助國王。基特族為貝奧武夫舉辦了一個盛大的葬禮。他的遺體被放在火葬用的樹枝中點火焚燒。骨灰就放在懸崖上的一座古墳中，眺望著大海。來往航行的水手都會看到最偉大的戰士之墓。基特人為了失去他們偉大的領袖而哀痛，他們也害怕，因為沒有貝奧武夫的保護，他們的未來顯得渺茫慘淡。

答　案

一、閱讀測驗 (Reading Comprehension)

答　1. C　　2. A　　3. B　　4. D

解析：

1. 文中提到了貝奧武夫和格倫戴爾的母親戰鬥時，一直無法用自己的劍傷害到牠，後來貝奧武夫看到有一把巨大的劍懸掛在旁邊的牆上，他取下那把劍之後才砍傷了格倫戴爾母親的脖子，最後殺死了牠，由此可以得知貝奧武夫並不是用自己的劍打敗格倫戴爾的母親，因此答案為 (C)。

2. 由文中的內容可以得知，海格拉克是貝奧武夫的叔叔，因此 (A) 為正確答案。

3. 貝奧武夫在晚年時為了捍衛他的國家而和一頭龍戰鬥，在過程當中，他的脖子被那頭龍咬了一口，後來貝奧武夫就死於這個有毒的傷口，因此答案為 (B)。

4. 綜觀整篇文章，可以看出文章的目的在於簡短地介紹貝奧武夫的生平以及他的英勇事蹟，因此答案為 (D)。

二、字彙填充 (Fill in the Blanks)

答　1. courteous　　2. eloquent　　3. pledged

三、引導式翻譯 (Guided Translation)

答　1. flew; into; a; rage　　2. dived; into　　3. burned; to; the; ground

Chapter 2
Utopia

烏托邦

　　湯瑪斯・摩爾遊歷歐洲，遇到了很多奇妙的人士。不過，一次在比利時的巧合會面，造成了他最具衝擊性的發現。摩爾見到彼得・蓋爾斯感到很高興，他是安特衛普城的市民。蓋爾斯性情開朗並且博學多聞，他介紹摩爾認識一名老者，叫做拉斐爾・希斯拉德，他是一位睿智並且因遊歷各地而見多識廣的人。他有著長鬍子，一張老邁並因日晒而黝黑的臉龐。

　　希斯拉德對於文明與政治有很多想法，也不吝於分享。當三個人在討論這些想法時，對於每個人在群體中所扮演積極角色應盡的義務，產生了激烈的辯論。摩爾與蓋爾斯認為一個有經驗且正直的人應該要為他的國家與族群服務。摩爾甚至認為，希斯拉德這樣的智慧對國家與王族來說會是最有用的顧問。對有權的人進諫忠言，讓他們知曉這些忠告，希斯拉德可對國家產生最大的幫助。

　　希斯拉德拒絕聽從摩爾與蓋爾斯的建議擔任公職，他批評他所觀察到現在很多歐洲國家的政治現狀。希斯拉德認為，各國君王不為人民福祉著想，處心積慮發動戰爭，征討更多領土來壯大自己的勢力。錢財與資源都投注在這些毫無意義的努力上，讓國家陷入貧困與饑餓的惡性循環中。希斯拉德也批評了國王濫用死刑來懲治罪犯，還有實行圈地運動，禁止人民進入共有的領地。

　　摩爾認為，像希斯拉德這樣的哲學家，應該要在人群之間落實他們的理念，而不是只有思考與現實無關的崇高理論。政治系統的改革很慢，權宜之計只有在這有缺陷的系統裡繼續努力，把體制改得更好，而不是從頭開始。

　　摩爾、蓋爾斯以及希斯拉德停下了他們的對話，享受了一頓愉悅的晚餐。在他們繼續討論的時候，話題轉到了希斯拉德最近旅行去過的烏托邦。在世界各地接觸過各式各樣的族群之後，希斯拉德迫不及待地要分享在烏托邦看到的特殊文化。

　　烏托邦是一個新月形狀的島嶼，在兩端各有一條波濤洶湧的狹窄海道。在島的內部是一個平靜的海港，有和緩的海浪與沙岸，而在外部則面對著廣闊大海的島嶼，島上特有的是崎嶇的岩岸。這樣的地理形勢讓外人很難進入島嶼內部，除非有島上的住民親自引導。

　　烏托邦的城市與鄉村之間相互依賴，有著密切的聯繫。在這個國家中，每塊田地都有超過四十位以上的人在耕作。每年都有一定數量的城市居民來到鄉村，接替前一年在農田裡工作的人。這樣，所有的烏托邦人民皆學習重要的耕作技術，沒有一個特定族群會終其一生陷於耕作的種種雜事而感到力不從心。這裡有五十四座城

市，彼此之間步行就可以相互來往。艾默若是烏托邦的首都。這個城市到處都有盛產水果、蔬菜以及藥草的園子。街道寬廣而整潔，一排一排的房屋排列整齊。任何房子裡都沒有私人的財產。事實上，每十年烏托邦的居民就會換房子。

每年，每三十個家庭或一個農場都會選出一位執政官來代表他們。這個行政體制藉由一個祕密選舉選出一位終身職的地方法官，其他的行政單位則是執政一年。所有關於這個國家的議題都必須在議會上經過三天的討論，任何在議會廳外討論國家議題的行為都視為可處以死刑的重罪，這條法律旨在防止地方法官與外人共謀壓榨人民，或是把烏托邦的共和政體改為專制。

比起世界其他地方，黃金與珠寶在烏托邦有完全不同的價值。烏托邦的人民重視鐵，因為這是鑄造生存工具的重要物質。他們不珍惜金子，金子反而被用來製造家用器具，像夜壺。他們收集海邊的珍珠，送給小孩子當作玩具，好像這不過就是石頭。珍貴的珠寶被視為一般物品，這也是它們本來的價值，不過就是地球上的一種物質。

烏托邦的人民都有學習農作的技術，除了耕作之外，他們還學習石工、木工與紡織。每位烏托邦的男女都各自專精一項工藝，他們工作的時間被嚴格限制在一天六個小時之內。其他的時間都要用來休息、飲食或者從事休閒活動。很多烏托邦人會參與各種主題的講座像是彈奏樂器或照顧花園，目的只在於自娛或刺激知識成長罷了。

所有的男女自小都受到音樂、邏輯、算數與幾何的教育。他們在天文學方面也受到啟發，會觀察月亮的陰晴圓缺，還有天上的星星與太陽。然而，學習美德與生活的快樂才是他們主要的追求。烏托邦人對於探討快樂的真諦非常感興趣，經常會問這樣的問題：「生活要如何才能快樂？」他們相信，人性的主要訴求，就是為個人帶來健康與舒適的生活，並且將他人的痛苦與災禍減到最低。為了自己的快樂而讓別人不開心，這本身就是錯誤的行為。

烏托邦人不把奴隸制度當社會制度的一環，但將戰俘與犯過重罪的人充當奴隸。奴隸會為整個國家做底層的工作，像是屠宰。

18 歲以上的人才能結婚。婚前性行為被嚴格禁止，如果發生則會受到嚴格懲罰，因為大家相信要是每個人都沉溺在這樣的惡習裡，很少人會選擇結婚。不過，他們的習俗會讓準新郎與準新娘在同意結婚之前，彼此裸體相見，因為他們相信，婚姻要長久，雙方就要知道面對的是怎樣的人。大部分的婚姻都是至死不渝，除非發生通姦，或是雙方都同意離婚，但這種情況非常少見。議會除非仔細考慮過雙方的說詞，不會輕易同意離婚，因為這裡的人相信，惡意拋棄自己的配偶，是很殘忍的行為。

烏托邦人憎恨戰爭，也盡力避免戰爭。不過，他們仍有軍隊，軍隊中有男有女，日夜操練，以備不時之需。他們介入戰爭的可能情況就是為了保衛國家，為了替友邦抵抗外來的侵犯，或是為了讓某個族群可以脫離暴政。除此之外，他們都覺得戰爭是一件自負而可惡的事情。

關於宗教，多數的烏托邦人相信只有一個神。這個主導的力量，全宇宙的創造者，被視為世界的主宰。然而，其他烏托邦人崇拜太陽、星星、月亮以及其他宗教象徵。這個共和政體的其中一條古老律法就說明了所有的人都有選擇信仰的自由。要是一個人想要其他人跟隨自己的信仰，就必須以和平尊重的手段來進行，絕對不可以使用暴力。

在聽完希斯拉德對烏托邦與這個國家特殊風俗的陳述之後，摩爾並沒有完全對烏托邦的體制信服。摩爾相信，沒有金錢的支持，共和政體真正的榮耀與光芒是無法存在的。然而，他認為烏托邦的特色是很好的，希望歐洲可以採納烏托邦的特色。

答案

一、閱讀測驗 (Reading Comprehension)

答　1. A　　2. C　　3. B　　4. D

解析：

1. 本文的主要目的是向讀者介紹一個想像且獨特的社會，故答案為 (A)。

2. 希斯拉德本身曾經去過烏托邦、很樂於分享他的想法和意見、經常到處遊歷，因此選項 A、B、D 的內容都是錯誤的。而由第三段的內容得知，他不願意進入公職去服務，因此 (C) 的敘述是正確的。

3. 由文中得知，外人難以進入烏托邦的原因，是由於其特殊的地理環境所致，並不是因為周圍有建造高牆，因此 (B) 的敘述內容是不正確的。

4. 希斯拉德在描述烏托邦時的順序是地理位置、政治制度、職業分配、教育、婚姻、宗教等，因此正確答案為 (D)。

二、字彙填充 (Fill in the Blanks)

答　1. obligation　　2. tyranny　　3. integrity

三、引導式翻譯 (Guided Translation)

答　1. goes; to; great; lengths　　2. no; fewer; than　　3. from; scratch

Chapter 3
Doctor Faustus

浮士德

　　浮士德博士生於德國的一個貧窮的家庭。他天資聰穎，在威騰堡一間有名的大學取得教職。他主要的研究領域是神學，得到了神學博士學位。浮士德接下來在其他的領域也成為專家，成為一個有名的學者。

　　可是，儘管學富五車，浮士德並不滿足現狀。他精通邏輯學，藥學，法律以及神學。然而，他仍然遭受到凡人的各種限制。基督信仰中，所有人類皆為罪人，只能因為對神的忠誠而得救，對此，浮士德嗤之以鼻。他認為自己的道德比一般人還要高尚。浮士德想要他身邊的人所得不到的權力與歡愉。因此，為了滿足自己的慾望，這個負有盛名的學者轉向研究黑巫術。他決定要邀請他的朋友范爾德斯與柯內里奧斯共進晚餐，這兩個人都是施展黑巫術的人。

　　在等待的時候，善天使與惡天使來拜訪他。善天使懇求他，要他避免接觸黑巫術，不然他將會永遠被詛咒。惡天使則鼓勵他深究這門魔法，來得到神一般的力量。浮士德無法抵抗惡天使的誘惑，天真地想像自己有朝一日可以實現自己所有的慾望。

　　他的朋友來了以後，他們就施展某種咒語，讓浮士德可以召喚神靈，服從他的命令。他們離開以後，浮士德決定要使用這新學來的知識。他開始施展咒語，邪惡的梅菲斯托費勒斯隨即現身。這讓浮士德對於他的魔法信心大增，他要求惡魔服從他的命令。可是，梅菲斯托費勒斯說，這需要先取得他的主人路西法的允許。

　　他告訴浮士德說，路西法曾經是上帝最鍾愛的天使，可是這天使卻組織了一個叛軍背叛上帝。因此，路西法與他的追隨者就被永世打入地獄，浮士德爭論說，梅菲斯托費勒斯既然在他的書房裡，就不會在地獄。梅菲斯托費勒斯回應：「這就是地獄，我也沒出來過。」因為地獄就是被隔離在天堂之外的狀態。這惡魔甚至警告浮士德，不要因為向路西法尋求力量，而危害到自己的靈魂。

　　可是，浮士德拒絕相信地獄的恐怖，要求梅菲斯托費勒斯向路西法提出一個交易。浮士德答應給路西法自己的靈魂，只要梅菲斯托費勒斯可以在二十四年裡都充當他的奴僕。梅菲斯托費勒斯答應在午夜時帶來路西法的回覆。

　　善天使與惡天使又出現了。浮士德拒絕善天使要他「多想想天堂」的忠告，反而被惡天使說服，「相信榮耀與財富」。接著，梅菲斯托費勒斯回來了。他告訴浮士德說，路西法答應了這筆交易，代價就是浮士德的靈魂。除此之外，浮士德必須要以自己的血簽下契約。

浮士德很樂意地割開自己的手臂，拿血簽下契約。然而，他的血突然停止流動，好像抗拒這樁邪惡的行為。梅菲斯托費勒斯去拿了一些火來，融化了浮士德的血液。儘管發生這樣隱晦的警告，浮士德堅持繼續交易。當梅菲斯托費勒斯帶回來一盆火以後，浮士德就完成了簽字。他接下來看到他的手臂上出現了拉丁字「*homo, fuge*」，意思是「人類，快逃」，他覺得很驚異。浮士德無所顧忌地忽略掉這個清楚的警告，執著地完成這個契約，因為他相信「地獄只是個寓言」。

　　因此，藉由使喚梅菲斯托費勒斯，浮士德沉迷於各式各樣的享受，他也命令惡魔滿足他對於宇宙的好奇心。然而，當他問起誰創造了這個世界，梅菲斯托費勒斯不回答了。他說，他只能回答沒有違背地獄王國的問題，而且，浮士德應該多想想關於他自己墮落下去的狀況。浮士德警覺起來，並且思索著，他是不是有機會重回上帝身邊。

　　善天使與惡天使又出現了。惡天使說，「太遲了。」可是好天使說，「不會太遲的，只要浮士德懺悔。」浮士德慌了，祈求耶穌基督，「救救浮士德墮落的靈魂吧！」這次，路西法親自現身。浮士德被他聲色俱厲嚇到了。路西法警告浮士德，提到耶穌基督，就會破壞他們的契約。當浮士德發誓「絕對不再仰望天堂」，路西法答應給他巨大的報償。

　　為了要讓浮士德相信，這個契約對他有利，路西法召喚了七大罪，他們展示在浮士德面前，表現出來罪惡的歡愉。浮士德說，這個展示讓他的靈魂愉悅，重申他對契約的忠誠，然後路西法就離去了。

　　現在，浮士德完全掌握了他的魔法力量。站在奧林帕斯山頂，藉由觀看雲層，星體與天上的星星，他發掘了天文學的祕密。他的馬車是龍在拉的，坐在這臺雙輪馬車裡，他環遊世界，接著，在梅菲斯托費勒斯的陪伴下，他決定遊歷世界上最偉大的國度。

　　他們的第一個目的地，就是教宗在羅馬的宗教法庭。他們裝扮成兩個樞機主教，拜訪教宗。教宗要他們安排布魯諾的行刑，因為德國皇帝有意要把布魯諾扶植為教宗。可是，浮士德與梅菲斯托費勒斯幫助他逃到德國。後來，在一個宴會上，兩位真正的樞機主教就被羞辱，因為他們完全對教宗的命令不知情。他們被控反叛，並且被判死刑。

　　浮士德命令梅菲斯托費勒斯把他變成隱形。他就可以戲弄教宗，偷拿他的食物與酒。所有的賓客相信鬧鬼了，教宗就叫來教士驅鬼。浮士德看到教宗畫十字，就覺得很生氣。當教士們趕到，開始驅鬼的時候，浮士德與梅菲斯托費勒斯在教堂裡面丟下煙火，然後就逃跑了。

　　接下來，浮士德拜訪德國皇帝的宮廷裡。皇帝很感謝他們，因為他們救了布魯諾。浮士德感到受寵若驚，在皇帝要求要看到亞歷山大大帝與他的愛人時，浮士德樂於聽

命。浮士德施咒，這位古代的希臘皇帝就現身了。整個宮廷看到亞歷山大殺了波斯大流士並且把他的皇冠戴在自己愛人的頭上。這些靈魂接著跟德國皇帝致意，然後就消失了。

浮士德也對人施以惡毒的惡作劇來自娛。有一天，他遇到一個馬商，就把馬便宜地賣給他。他告訴這個受害者說，不要騎馬入水。不過，馬商不管浮士德的警告，這匹馬就變成了一束稻草。他很生氣，就在浮士德睡覺的時候攻擊他。馬商拉浮士德的腳的時候，這腳掉了下來，馬商就把這腳偷走了。接著，他看到浮士德兩腳完好如初，覺得很驚訝，他知道自己又被愚弄了。

聽到浮士德惡劣的言行，有一個聖潔的老人試著要拯救浮士德的靈魂。他警告浮士德，「遠離這個該死的黑巫術」，不然，就來不及要求上帝的寬恕了。他說，仍然有一個天使徘徊在浮士德的頭上，可以繼續在浮士德的靈魂裡面灌注寬容。浮士德動搖了，開始後悔他跟路西法的愚蠢交易。梅菲斯托費勒斯這時介入，指控浮士德背叛他。他威脅說如果浮士德轉向上帝，就要把他撕成碎片。浮士德受到驚嚇，重申自己對路西法的誓約。

當契約到期的日子接近時，浮士德要求梅菲斯托費勒斯帶來傳說中的海倫，當作自己的伴侶。當她出現時，浮士德完全被她的美貌給征服，他呼喊著，「這就是那出動了上千艘船的容顏嗎？」浮士德要求她「用一個吻讓我得到永生」。然後，他就吻了海倫，希望自己永遠跟她在一起。

不過，這是不可能的。浮士德二十四年的合約期限已經到期了。在這最後一個晚上，三個學者來拜訪浮士德，他們看到浮士德既蒼白又虛弱，覺得很驚奇。浮士德告訴他們自己與路西法的交易，他說他將要「永世墮入地獄」。學者催促他禱告以獲得拯救，可是浮士德知道他的禱告不會有任何效用。

善天使與惡天使最後一次拜訪浮士德，善天使哀嘆浮士德墮入了永恆的折磨，而惡天使則是把地獄的恐怖顯現在浮士德的眼前。接著，時鐘敲響十一下。浮士德急切地祈求時間能慢下來，祈求耶穌基督可以拯救他。

午夜來臨，可怕的雷擊降臨，惡魔來帶走了浮士德。過了幾天，學者們回到這裡來，他們聽到了在那暴風雨的時候，哭喊求救的聲音。他們找到了浮士德的屍體，已被撕為碎片。基於對於同為學者的敬意，他們收集好浮士德的殘肢，在一個肅穆的葬禮上埋葬浮士德。

一、閱讀測驗 (Reading Comprehension)

答 1. C　　2. A　　3. B　　4. D

解析：

1. 浮士德之所以想要學會使用黑巫術，是因為他不滿足於現狀、過於貪婪，而且認為自己在道德上比其他人都更加優越所致，故答案為 (C)。

2. 在與魔鬼的合約快到期之前，浮士德要求梅菲斯托費勒斯把古希臘第一美女海倫帶來，結果他對她一見鍾情，也想與她永遠在一起，故答案為 (A)。

3. 在與魔鬼簽約之後，其實浮士德曾經幾度萌生後悔的念頭，因此可以得知 (B) 的敘述是錯誤的。

4. 由整篇文章的內容可以得知，全文的寓意在於勸導人們不應該太過於自私，而且也應該把自身的力量用於造福人群，而非僅為一己之私，故答案為 (D)。

二、字彙填充 (Fill in the Blanks)

答 1. intervene　　2. treason　　3. renowned

三、引導式翻譯 (Guided Translation)

答 1. cast; a; spell　　2. specializes; in　　3. ran; off; with

Chapter 4
Hamlet

哈姆雷特

　　在德國的威登堡念書時，王子哈姆雷特收到父親，也就是丹麥國王，去世的消息。因此，他回到艾爾西諾堡的丹麥宮廷參加葬禮。哈姆雷特原是王位的繼承人，然而，他的母親葛楚德皇后很快地與他的叔叔克勞迪亞斯訂婚了。他們兩個月後就結婚了，所以，克勞迪亞斯成為國王，哈姆雷特留在丹麥參加婚禮與加冕典禮。對於母親這麼快再婚，哈姆雷特覺得很痛苦。除此之外，他也對克勞迪亞斯感到不滿，他覺得叔叔遠遠比不上自己的父親。

　　在宮廷上，哈姆雷特忠誠的朋友何瑞修告訴丹麥王子說，他跟幾個城堡守衛看到了一個鬼魂。他說，這鬼魂看起來很像是哈姆雷特的父親。哈姆雷特當晚就和他們一起去城牆調查這個鬼魂。當鬼魂出現時，哈姆雷特急忙前去見他。這鬼魂表明他就是哈姆雷特父親的靈魂，而且他是被克勞迪亞斯殺害的。大家都以為，他是在花園睡覺的時候，被毒蛇咬到而死。事實上，他的弟弟悄悄溜進來，在國王的耳朵裡倒進了毒藥。鬼魂命令哈姆雷特要「為他這樁殘忍且違反倫常的謀殺復仇」。哈姆雷特發誓，他會殺了他犯罪的叔叔，答應要「飛快地前去報仇」。可是，哈姆雷特也擔憂，「在這混亂的世道中」，太過武斷的作為會有問題。他也因為母親的作為感到悲傷與憤怒，失去了行動的能力，並且憤恨地說，他「生下來就是為了要撥亂反正」。

　　哈姆雷特並沒有立刻行動，內心混亂的王子決定要裝瘋。他想要騙過國王，避免讓國王把他當作威脅。然而，克勞迪亞斯產生了懷疑，因為哈姆雷特在婚禮上表達了他的敵意。克勞迪亞斯要求他的大臣，坡洛尼厄斯，就近觀察哈姆雷特。坡洛尼厄斯反對哈姆雷特對他女兒奧菲莉亞的感情，並警告女兒不要給哈姆雷特追求的機會。當奧菲莉亞告訴父親說，哈姆雷特來看過她，並且行為怪異，坡洛尼厄斯認定，奧菲莉亞拒絕哈姆雷特的追求，造成了他的瘋狂。然而，國王並不相信坡洛尼厄斯的講法，仍然小心提防著哈姆雷特。

　　一個巡迴的演藝團來到了丹麥宮廷。哈姆雷特迎接了他們，並且要他們朗誦一齣有名戲碼裡面的臺詞，他看到這些演員只因想像而激起了表演的熱情，覺得很慚愧，自責自己卻沒有對一樁實際的罪行採取行動。哈姆雷特指示演藝團，在為宮廷表演戲劇時加上一幕新的劇本。在這新的戲碼中，一個國王被他的姪子在耳朵裡面灌注毒藥謀殺。哈姆雷特預期，他的叔叔會因為這齣「捕鼠器」顯現出罪惡感的反應，證明鬼魂說的話是正確的。然而，王子又顯得猶豫不決，再次延遲了他的復仇。

在表演開始之前，哈姆雷特突然陷入了絕望。他問自己，「生存還是毀滅，這是個值得思考的問題。」這意味著他在思考自殺。哈姆雷特在思考的是一個嚴峻的選擇。他應該要以自殺來結束這「如海一般浩瀚的苦難」嗎？或者，他要努力奮戰來克服這些困難？他做了決定，自殺無法解決問題，因為死亡是一個「未經探索的領域」。他害怕他有可能會進入一個跟他現在狀況一樣可怕的來世。

因此，哈姆雷特出席了演出。在演出謀殺場景之後，克勞迪亞斯呼喊著「給我光」然後就急忙離開了。哈姆雷特現在很確定，他的叔叔是有罪的。而國王這時也知道，哈姆雷特對他產生了威脅。這場戲忠實呈現了他殺害了自己的兄弟，同時，這齣戲也包含了一個潛在的威脅：哈姆雷特安排國王被姪子殺掉。

克勞迪亞斯決定要把哈姆雷特送去英國執行外交任務，實際上是想要殺掉哈姆雷特。國王召來羅森克蘭茲與吉爾登斯坦。他們原來是哈姆雷特的舊識，現在卻成了國王的手下。克勞迪亞斯利用他們來監視哈姆雷特。他告訴他們，準備好跟王子一起去英國。

當他們離開之後，國王突然之間感覺到一陣很強的罪惡感。他跪下來，祈求上天的原諒。這時，哈姆雷特進到大廳，看到國王正在祈禱，卻沒有動手殺他。王子說服自己說，如果這時下手殺他，國王就會進入天堂。哈姆雷特想要送國王進地獄，所以就暫且饒了他一命，離開了。可是，克勞迪亞斯這時也停止了祈禱，並且了解到，他絕對不會改變自己的罪惡本性。

接著，哈姆雷特前往皇后的寢宮見他的母親。在寢宮裡，坡洛厄亞斯正在勸皇后好好掌控她的兒子。在大臣聽到哈姆雷特來的時候，他就躲在幕簾的後面。哈姆雷特想要告訴皇后，父親是被謀殺的。可是，當皇后因為他的怒意而飽受驚嚇時，坡洛尼厄斯大叫求救。哈姆雷特匆忙拔劍刺向布簾，大臣就死了。哈姆雷特以為布簾後面就是國王。這時，鬼魂再次出現，只有哈姆雷特能看到。鬼魂責怪哈姆雷特忘記了他的誓言。

當國王發現坡洛尼厄斯被殺害之後，他堅持哈姆雷特立刻離開，前往英國。他欺騙羅森克蘭茲與吉爾登史坦，跟他們說，哈姆雷特殺害了坡洛尼厄斯，眾怒已犯，要保護他不受傷害，這是必要的。可是，在他送給英國國王的信裡面，他要求英國國王將哈姆雷特處以死刑。

在哈姆雷特要上船時，他遇到了一個挪威部隊的軍官，這個軍官說，他正在尋求福丁布拉斯王子與他的軍隊的同意，通過丹麥領土去到波蘭。福丁布拉斯與波蘭王有過爭端，就只是為了一塊不起眼的領土有所爭議，福丁布拉斯王子下定決心要周旋到底。聽到這樣的消息，哈姆雷特再次對自己感到憤怒。因為，對照這忠誠的王子，儘管哈姆雷特已經有很強烈的動機採取報復的行動，他卻什麼都還沒有做。

哈姆雷特離開以後，坡洛尼厄斯的兒子，萊厄提斯，從巴黎求學回來。他急著要為父親的死報仇。克勞迪亞斯見過他，並且跟他說，自己與坡洛尼厄斯的死無關。接著，萊厄提斯的妹妹，奧菲莉亞登場，情況非常糟糕。她會發瘋是因為父親的死造成精神的創傷，以及哈姆雷特的作為。萊厄提斯想要立刻復仇，而克勞迪雅斯答應要為他討回公道。

　　當國王收到哈姆雷特要返國的消息，非常震驚。這表示國王原先的計畫失敗了。哈姆雷特先拆開了國王託付給羅森克蘭茲與吉爾登斯坦的信，發現了克勞迪亞斯要刺殺他的陰謀。接著，海盜打劫了這艘船，哈姆雷特就被抓住，王子說服他們帶他回丹麥，回國後他會重賞這些海盜。

　　萊厄提斯要求與哈姆雷特決鬥。他的憤怒在他知道妹妹因悲傷而死之後與日俱增。克勞迪亞斯說服萊厄提斯交給自己來計畫刺殺哈姆雷特，因為哈姆雷特在民間很受到歡迎，如果萊厄提斯殺了哈姆雷特，可能輿論不容。萊厄提斯聽從國王的計謀，並且同意要出手援助。

　　克勞迪亞斯派了一個侍從去邀請哈姆雷特與萊厄提斯進行鬥劍比賽。侍從告訴哈姆雷特，國王已經下注賭哈姆雷特會贏。因為這是公開的比賽，所以雙方只能使用鈍劍，對此哈姆雷特沒有起疑。然而，萊厄提斯的劍尖端已經塗上了毒藥。他會假裝不小心用力過猛，刺傷哈姆雷特。國王也準備了一杯毒酒，讓他在比賽的時候喝下去。

　　就這樣，哈姆雷特與萊厄提斯開始了比賽。在比賽的中場休息時，皇后給哈姆雷特一杯酒，哈姆雷特先拒絕了，因為他想趕快得到勝利。接著大事不妙，皇后自己喝了一口毒酒，國王也來不及阻止。同時，萊厄提斯與哈姆雷特越打越激烈並刺傷了哈姆雷特。可是，他們的劍在兩人扭打的時候互換，哈姆雷特也以那把上了毒的劍刺傷萊厄提斯。

　　皇后發出慘叫，因為她喝了毒酒，快要死去。接著她倒地死亡。而萊厄提斯臨死前，跟受傷的哈姆雷特說出國王的陰謀。撐著最後一口氣，哈姆雷特以毒劍刺傷國王，並強迫他喝下毒酒。克勞迪亞斯倒在皇后旁邊，一命嗚呼。而哈姆雷特與萊厄提斯在嚥氣之前，也原諒了彼此。

　　最後，福丁布拉斯王子來到了宮廷裡，那時他剛戰勝了波蘭，正要打道回府。看到這個混亂的場面，他宣布自己成為丹麥的國王，因為所有的貴族都已死去。可是，他想到哈姆雷特以這樣的方式死去，就覺得很遺憾，因為他相信哈姆雷特原本會是個好的國王。因此，他下令以全軍禮的方式下葬哈姆雷特，讓哈姆雷特得到應得的榮耀。

一、閱讀測驗 (Reading Comprehension)

答　1. A　　2. B　　3. D　　4. C

解析：

1. 哈姆雷特雖然從父親的鬼魂那得知他父親是被叔叔殺死的，但他一直猶豫不決，不確定這是不是事實，所以要求在一場宮廷上演的演出中加入一幕，測試他叔叔的反應，並以此種方式來確認他父親是不是真的被他叔叔所殺死，故答案為 (A)。

2. 當哈姆雷特說出這句話的時候，他的意思是指他自己陷入了很大的痛苦與絕望當中，甚至考慮要自殺，因此答案為 (B)。

3. 哈姆雷特最後是用那把有毒的劍傷了他的叔叔，並且強迫他叔叔喝下毒酒，使他叔叔毒發身亡，為自己的父親報了仇，因此 (D) 的敘述才是正確的。

4. 綜觀全文，哈姆雷特之所以無法早日成功為他父親復仇，最大原因是因為他一直優柔寡斷、遲遲無法下決定，才會落得最後也丟掉自己生命的下場，因此讀者們從這個故事中可以學到的教訓，就是在面對艱難的處境時，我們應該要果決地採取行動，不要錯失良機，故答案為 (C)。

二、字彙填充 (Fill in the Blanks)

答　1. pirates　　2. expired　　3. passionate

三、引導式翻譯 (Guided Translation)

答　1. blamed; for　　2. quarrel; with; over　　3. pretends; to

翻 譯

傲慢與偏見

　　多金的單身漢查爾斯‧賓利租下奈德菲莊園的一座宅邸時，班奈特太太很興奮。班奈特家族住在鄰近的龍伯恩莊園。她希望自己的五個女兒能有一個嫁給他。

　　班奈特太太希望她的女兒能嫁到好人家，因為她丈夫的莊園屬於限定繼承。意思是龍伯恩莊園必須由最親近的男性親屬來繼承。班奈特太太害怕她的女兒們後半輩子都得依靠其他男性親屬的接濟。班奈特家附近的梅里屯要舉辦一個舞會，而賓利先生會出席，班奈特太太非常高興。賓利先生出席舞會的時候有一個富有的朋友陪同，他叫做費茲威廉‧達西先生。

　　在那天晚上，賓利先生溫和的性格讓他很受歡迎。可是，達西先生卻因為傲慢的態度引起大家的不滿。班奈特家的大女兒——珍，吸引了賓利先生的注意。他鼓勵自己的朋友去跟珍的妹妹伊莉莎白跳舞。達西先生說：「她不夠漂亮，無法吸引我。」伊莉莎白偷聽到這樣的對話，覺得達西先生是一個傲慢而難相處的人。

　　珍收到了賓利先生妹妹的邀請，前往奈德菲莊園一起共進晚餐，這時賓利先生一行人正在梅里屯拜訪軍官，這讓班奈特太太非常高興。班奈特太太決定要用馬送她的女兒前往，而不是用馬車。她期待會下雨。珍這樣就必須在奈德菲莊園過夜，然後又會再度碰到賓利先生。班奈特太太的計畫成功了。下雨了，珍淋濕了。可是，她也因此得了重感冒，必須待下來幾天。班奈特太太派伊莉莎白去照顧她。

　　在這期間，賓利先生與珍越來越親近。而連伊莉莎白自己都不知道的是，達西先生也被她所吸引。他喜歡伊莉莎白的獨立與聰慧。一天晚上，當她因為當時在梅里屯的舞會自尊受傷而拒絕與他跳舞時，達西先生對她獨立的性格又更加欽佩。

　　班奈特姊妹回到龍伯恩莊園，班奈特先生的表親威廉‧柯林斯先生來拜訪他們，他是這莊園的繼承人。他正要前往一個教堂接受新職。柯林斯先生被任命為凱瑟琳‧迪‧包爾女伯爵教區的新教長，這位女伯爵也是達西先生的阿姨。伊莉莎白覺得柯林斯先生是個既高傲又愚昧的人。他來訪的主要原因，就是要利用自己的社會地位，把班奈特姊妹之一收為自己的妻子。

　　在柯林斯先生到達的第二天，柯林斯先生陪伴班奈特姊妹前去梅里屯。在那兒他們碰到了一個軍官，這人對班奈特的兩個妹妹，凱瑟琳與莉迪雅很友善。他把她們介紹給一個叫做喬治‧韋克翰的人。這人剛加入軍隊。姊妹們都很喜歡這個魅力十足又很英俊的軍官。接著，賓利先生與達西先生騎馬經過，跟所有人致意。伊莉莎白注意到，韋克翰先生與達西先生的互動很冷漠。

隨後的會面之中，伊莉莎白很喜歡韋克翰先生。她向韋克翰先生問起達西先生。韋克翰說，他的父親在潘伯利做過僕役，那是達西先生亡父的領地。他說，達西先生的父親待他有如己出，並且答應要給他一筆遺產，讓他有固定的收入，可是達西先生在父親過世之後拒絕給他這筆遺產。韋克翰先生認為，達西先生的父親對自己的關愛，讓達西先生很嫉妒。他的這般陳述，更加強了伊莉莎白對達西先生的敵意。

柯林斯先生本來很喜歡珍，可是他後來聽到珍可能會嫁給賓利先生，因此他向伊莉莎白求婚，覺得她一定會接受。然而，在兩人獨處的時候，伊莉莎白很有禮貌卻很堅決地拒絕了柯林斯先生，她說兩人並不合適。班奈特太太很生氣。她相信自己的女兒應該為了班奈特家族的未來嫁給這個繼承人。柯林斯先生後來跟伊莉莎白的好朋友夏綠蒂求婚，她就住在附近的梅里屯。夏綠蒂接受了，因為柯林斯先生會給她穩定的生活。

賓利先生因為工作的關係必須前往倫敦，這讓班奈特太太很失望。接著，班奈特太太的哥哥賈丁納先生帶著妻子來訪。他們邀請珍一起去倫敦。伊莉莎白希望她能在那兒遇到賓利先生。賈丁納太太注意到伊莉莎白對韋克翰先生的好感。她覺得很疑惑，警告她說，這男人太窮了，嫁給他不是一個理性的決定。可是，伊莉莎白下定決心，不要讓自己因為對方缺乏財富而產生偏見。

幾個禮拜後，伊莉莎白接到一封珍從倫敦寄來的信。信上寫說她去拜訪賓利小姐，可是並沒有受到歡迎。珍相信，賓利小姐希望她的哥哥能娶達西先生的妹妹，因為達西小姐更富有。因此，她想阻撓珍與賓利先生的會面。

三月，夏綠蒂的父母，威廉先生與盧卡斯女士，邀請伊莉莎白一起旅行前往北方。在路途上，他們在柯林斯先生的教區拜訪了夏綠蒂與她的丈夫。在那兒，他們在羅森莊園中的鄉間大宅與凱瑟琳·迪·包爾女伯爵共餐。這時，達西先生也來拜訪他的阿姨。伊莉莎白與達西先生相互寒暄，可是她對達西先生並不友善。

因此，當達西先生突然向她求婚時，伊莉莎白非常驚訝，她很冷靜地拒絕了他。可是，當她發現達西先生承認自己阻止賓利先生與珍在倫敦見面，就變得非常憤怒。達西先生認為珍的背景與他的朋友不相配。伊莉莎白被這個人的社會偏見激怒，控訴他背叛了韋克漢先生。達西先生沒有回應就離開了。

第二天，伊莉莎白與達西先生在路上相遇，他給了她一封信就走開了。在信中，他說他的父親曾經留給韋克翰先生一千英鎊的遺產，並約定要他接受教堂的職位。然而，韋克翰先生對於這個工作並不感興趣，反而跟達西要求多兩千磅的遺產。他很快的就把錢揮霍光。達西先生接著解釋，他必須阻止韋克翰先生跟他的妹妹私奔，因為韋克翰只為了她的財富才想娶她。伊莉莎白這時對達西感到困惑，她也理解到，自己可能錯信了韋克翰先生。

當伊莉莎白回到龍伯恩莊園時，她向珍提到韋克翰先生的事，不過她們決定不要公開這件事。此時，韋克翰先生的單位來到了布萊頓。單位裡福斯特上校的妻子邀請莉迪雅‧班奈特到布萊頓一起度過這個夏天。莉迪雅很興奮，因為她可以去會見這些軍官。她的父親也准許她去，因為他相信上校與他的妻子會好好監護這個女孩子。

七月的時候，伊莉莎白與賈丁納夫婦一起前往德比郡旅遊。他們經過潘伯利，也就是達西先生的宅邸。他們以為達西先生不在，就去遊覽了這個莊園。伊莉莎白不禁想到，要是能跟達西先生結婚，一起生活在這個地方，不知會是什麼樣的光景。他們與達西先生的管家聊天，管家說，達西先生對他領地上的人都非常仁慈。

接著，達西先生突然出現了。他回來是為了準備迎接賓客。他邀請大家在第二天一起享用晚餐。賈丁納太太注意到達西先生愛上了伊莉莎白。當伊莉莎白回到旅館時，她接到了珍的來信。信上說，莉迪雅已經與韋克翰先生私奔了。

賈丁納先生與班奈特先生來到倫敦尋找這對情侶，後來賈丁納先生找到了他們。韋克翰先生堅持班奈特先生要保證給他一筆收入，他才會跟莉迪雅結婚。為了拯救家族的名聲，班奈特先生答應了，接著，賈丁納太太告訴伊莉莎白，達西先生也給了韋克翰先生一大筆錢。伊莉莎白因為達西先生的慷慨而感動，並且為之前拒絕他的求婚感到後悔。

最後，賓利先生回到奈德菲莊園，他拜訪了龍伯恩莊園，並留下來用晚餐。幾天後，他跟珍求婚，而珍也接受了。於此同時，伊莉莎白接受了凱瑟琳‧迪‧包爾女伯爵的一次意外拜訪。女伯爵懷疑達西先生愛上了伊莉莎白，不想讓他們兩個結婚。她說伊莉莎白的社會地位配不上她的姪子。伊莉莎白拒絕被這些說法影響，並說她有權決定自己要嫁給誰。

幾天之後，達西先生拜訪了奈德菲莊園。賓利先生與他一起拜訪住在龍伯恩莊園的班奈特一家。在路途上，伊莉莎白感謝達西先生幫助莉迪雅，並告訴他自己完全對他的想法改觀。達西先生這時再次求婚，而這次伊莉莎白也答應要嫁給他。因此，珍與伊莉莎白很開心地結婚了。伊莉莎白前往潘伯利，賓利先生在附近買了一個地產，因此這對姊妹可以常常見面。當然，班奈特太太非常地快樂。

答案

一、閱讀測驗 (Reading Comprehension)

答　1. A　　2. B　　3. C　　4. D

解析：

1. 在本故事中曾多次提及，那個時代的長輩在考量可能的結婚對象時，往往優先考慮對方的社會地位與財富，因此答案為 (A)。

2. 伊莉莎白一開始對於達西的印象很不好，她認為他是一個既自負又討厭的人，因此答案為 (B)。

3. 韋克翰是由柯林斯先生介紹給凱瑟琳和莉迪雅認識的，但是韋克翰與賓利之間並無任何關係，故 (C) 的敘述有誤，為本題的答案。

4. 故事內容可以得知，伊莉莎白是一個既聰明又獨立的女子，因此才會吸引達西的注意，故正確答案為 (D)。

二、字彙填充 (Fill in the Blanks)

答　1. arrogant　　2. mansion　　3. purchasing

三、引導式翻譯 (Guided Translation)

答　1. ran; away; with　　2. was; accused; of　　3. for; the; sake; of

Chapter 6
Frankenstein

科學怪人

　　一個英國的探險家，羅伯・華頓，正在北極進行一場遠征。他給妹妹寫了一封信，訴說旅途上的經歷與艱辛，他的第四封信提及了一些未曾預料的奇特事件。

　　他的船被冰包圍了。華頓在一群狗拖拉的雪橇上看到了一個巨大的身影。這個生物往北方疾行，很快地消失在視線中。晚上的時候，冰層破了，讓船可以移動。第二天早上，他聽到他的水手們在跟一個人講話，這人在冰層上搭著雪橇向他們的船漂過來。雖然這個人的身體狀況很差，他拒絕登船，直到知道了他們正在往北方航行。他告訴華頓，他正在追捕一個搭著另外一艘雪橇的龐大生物。華頓很為這個人的沉穩與決心折服，覺得這個人是一個「聖潔的流浪者」。這個旅行者要華頓聆聽他的故事。華頓把這個故事記錄在一個手稿裡，並把這手稿寄給他的妹妹。

　　這個男人叫做維克特・弗蘭肯斯坦。他說他生於瑞士的日內瓦。當他父親的姊姊過世時，整個家族照顧著她的女兒伊莉莎白。他的媽媽希望維克特有一天可以娶她的表妹。那時他的父親又生了兩個兒子。維克特也有一個很好的朋友，叫做亨利・克勒佛。維克特自小就培養了對自然科學的興趣。對於古代與中古時期召喚靈魂與創造生命的技術，他也同樣非常狂熱。他想要成為一個讓人類受益的偉大科學家。他後來被送去德國的因哥爾斯塔特念大學。在他要去念書前，他的母親生病並且過世了。

　　當他到達因哥爾斯塔特時，他遇到了一個教授，啟發他鑽研各種科學的能力。維克特相信這個相遇決定了他未來的命運。他夜以繼日的念書並做實驗。接著，維克特開始思索生命的起源。他研究屍體，了解屍體的腐化狀況。這次，他有了神奇的發現，他知道如何為死去的有機物回復生命。維克特產生了一個想法，他想創造一個人類。因為要啟動小器官的生命力比較困難，維克特決定要建構一個具有巨大形體的生命。他偷偷地收集了比較大的屍體殘肢與器官，在他自己房子裡的實驗室創造他的生物。

　　最後，他使用電力啟動創造物的生命。然而，在他成功的時刻，維克特理解到他創造了一個怪物。透過這個怪物的皮膚可以看到肌肉與跳動的血管，而且他的眼睛是恐怖的黃色。維克特衝出實驗室，後來，因為累壞了，就睡在自己的寢室裡。當他醒來，他發現這個怪物正靠近他的床，維克特逃到庭院裡，一直藏到早上。

　　第二天，維克特急忙回到城裡。在那裡，他看到從瑞士來了一輛馬車，他的朋友亨利・克勒佛走了出來。他來因哥爾斯塔特跟維克特一起念書。亨利看到維克特

的情況這麼糟糕，覺得很驚訝。接著，維克特就昏倒了，病了好幾個月。

當維克特說他決定要回到日內瓦時，他開始忘掉有關那個生物的事，而那怪物也消失了。然而，在要離開前去瑞士時，他接到父親的一封信。信上告訴維克特說，他的弟弟威廉被謀殺了。他的爸爸發現小男孩躺在草地上。他脖子上的痕跡說明他是被勒死的。

維克特立刻前往日內瓦。他回家之前，探訪了謀殺的地點。那是個夜晚，雷雨交加。當他到達的時候，一道雷電打下來，照亮了那個怪物的形體，而這怪物立刻消失在夜色裡。維克特相信他就是殺手。

儘管如此，他知道沒有人會相信他的想法，所以他保持沉默。接著，他家裡的女僕人賈絲婷被指控犯了這項謀殺罪。威廉總是隨身帶著母親的小畫像。而這畫像就在賈絲婷的口袋裡發現。維克特相信，這是那個怪物放的。賈絲婷被判有罪，並且遭到吊死。自那時開始，維克特就知道自己必須一生都背負這罪惡感，因為他創造的這個怪物才是「真正的謀殺者」。他下定決心，要找到並且毀掉這個怪物。

一天早上，維克特去爬山，因為他不想讓家人看到自己意志消沉的樣子。在山頂上，那個怪物靠近他，維克特攻擊了這怪物，可是怪物輕易地躲過了。他接下來要求維克特聽他講話。這怪物說，他想人類接受他，可是，每次人類看到他，就會恐懼地逃跑，接著開始獵殺他。因此，他必須要獨自逃走，生活在荒野裡。在孤獨的生活中，他心裡面滋長了對人類的恨意。他責怪維克特拋棄了他，所以，他對維克特的家人報仇。他要他的創造者同樣受到災禍。

這怪物要求維克特終止自己的孤獨，為他創造一個跟自己相像的妻子。他答應這樣他們就會遠離人類，不傷害人群。儘管這怪物做了可怕的事，維克特認為自己應該為怪物的福祉負起責任，因此答應了怪物的請求。而且他也必須保護人類不受怪物怒火的傷害。維克特聽說英國的科學家有辦法幫助他更快創造另外一個怪物。因此，他得到父親的允許，與他的朋友亨利前往英格蘭。維克特解釋說，他想要在與伊莉莎白安定下來之前，進行最後一次的旅行。

在倫敦，維克特得到了他需要的資訊。後來，維克特與亨利遊覽了英國，並拜訪了一個在蘇格蘭的朋友。維克特告訴亨利，他要獨自旅行一陣子，就前往一個北岸的離島。在那兒，他租了一個小屋，建立一個自己的實驗室。他收集了屍體，開始工作。一天晚上，怪物出現在實驗室的窗口，當他看到半完成的女性同伴時，他展現了一個可怕的笑容。

維克特在他眼中看到了邪惡的特質，就後悔當初的約定。他害怕自己會創造出兩個可怕的怪物，他們還會孕育可怕的後代，威脅到人類。他把這個未完成的身體撕毀。這怪物發出了「一聲絕望的邪惡怒吼」，並且留下了極為嚴厲的威脅：「我將於你的結婚之夜與你同在。」

維克特蒐集了肢體殘塊，然後從船上把它們丟入海中，便陷入了沈睡。當他醒來時，他發現自己已經飄離岸邊，迷航了。接著，他看到了陸地。他抵達了愛爾蘭。然而，當地的人對他很不友善，並抓住了他，在當地審判。

　　這個法官告訴維克特，維克特涉有重嫌，謀殺了一個被發現陳屍於附近海灘上的男人。維克特看到了這個屍體，並且很驚訝地發現這就是他的朋友亨利‧克勒佛。他猜想這是怪物做的。維克特被關起來，但是後來獲判無罪。證據顯示，在屍體被發現的時候，維克特還在島上。

　　維克特回到日內瓦之後娶了伊莉莎白。他下定決心，如果這怪物在結婚夜晚發動攻擊，他就會反擊。這對新人在艾維安的日內瓦湖上過夜。維克特全副武裝，帶著手槍與刀子，等待怪物的到來。然後，他聽到了一聲可怕的尖叫從伊麗莎白房間的方向傳來，他衝進房間，發現妻子已經死去，是被怪物勒死的。他從窗戶看到那怪物奸笑著，並嘲弄地指著伊莉莎白。維克特開了槍，但是怪物躲過了。

　　當維克特的父親聽到這個惡耗，就中風並且過世了。維克特因為神經緊張而崩潰。在恢復的過程中，他人生唯一的目標就是殺掉這個怪物。他在世界各地遊走，追捕他的敵人。而這怪物卻很享受這樣的追捕。最後，他來到北極，仍然追捕著這怪物直到最後冰層破了，華頓的船尋獲了維克特。

　　華頓寫信給他的妹妹，說維克特發了高燒，並且在說完故事之後就死去了。這些水手堅持要華頓開往英格蘭，因為天氣真的很糟糕。當這艘船啟航的時候，華頓聽到維克特屍體所在的那個艙房傳來聲音。他發現這怪物正在為他的創造者哀悼。

　　這個怪物告訴華頓，他對自己的行為感到很後悔，然而，在這世界上，沒有人比他更孤單更不幸。他告訴華頓，他會繼續向北航行，並且在冰漠中孤獨死去。接著他跳出船艙的窗戶。華頓看著他乘著筏向北方疾駛，消失在視線之外。

![答案]

一、閱讀測驗 (Reading Comprehension)

答 1. B　　2. B　　3. A　　4. D

解析：

1. 由全文內容可以得知，本文的主旨是在描述一位年輕的科學家維克特在創造出一個怪物後，因為後悔而想要毀掉這個怪物。因此答案為 (B)。

2. 由文中描述可以得知，由維克特所創造出來的怪物依序殺了威廉、亨利以及伊莉莎白，但是沒有殺死華頓，因此答案為 (B)。

3. 維克特原本答應要再創造一個怪物出來，但是他後來擔心兩個怪物之後可能會生下許多可怕的怪物，所以後來決定把未完成的第二個怪物撕成碎片、徹底摧毀，因此答案為 (A)。

4. 由文中怪物對維克特所說的話，以及最後那個怪物在維克特死後所做的事和所說的話來判斷，這個怪物事實上應該並不恨維克特，而且很渴望被維克特所接受，因此答案為 (D)。

二、字彙填充 (Fill in the Blanks)

答　1. manuscripts　　2. pistol　　3. solitude

三、引導式翻譯 (Guided Translation)

答　1. a; pack; of　　2. take; revenge; on　　3. Armed; with

孤雛淚

一天夜裡，一個懷孕的女人被發現躺在一個英國小鎮的街道上，沒有人知道她從哪裡來，所以她就被送到當地的濟貧院。在奮力生下一個男嬰後，這名筋疲力盡的女人哀求道：「在我死前，讓我看看孩子。」在孩子送到她面前時，她親吻了男嬰的額頭，然後死去。

這孩子被教區領事邦柏先生命名為奧利佛·崔斯特，並被送到附近的育幼院。在那裡，他度過了一個悲慘的童年，飽受虐待與飢餓。

在他 9 歲的時候，奧利佛開始在濟貧院工作。他被派去撿麻絮，也就是撿出舊麻繩裡面完整的繩線。這些小孩子沒有足夠的食物，卻要做這種粗重的工作，很多孩子一直在挨餓。一天晚上，他們選出奧利佛去請求更多食物。他向濟貧院的院長請求：「求求您，先生，我想要更多食物。」

院長很生氣，叫來了邦柏先生。奧利佛被毒打一頓，並且鎖在一個房間裡。教區領事出了五塊錢的酬金要把這個麻煩的孩子送走。索爾伯利先生是個殯葬業者，他接受了這筆酬金，因為他需要一個助理。

對奧利佛來說，這只是遷移到另外一個受苦的地方。他睡在棺材之間，並且吃狗吃剩的肉。奧利佛一直被另一個助理欺負，一個叫做諾亞·克雷波爾的小孩，年紀較長，他與女僕夏綠蒂嘲笑奧利佛。不過，索爾伯利先生喜歡奧利佛，讓他做自己的學徒。

這件事讓諾亞非常嫉妒，因此他繼續嘲笑奧利佛。有一天，他很殘酷地辱罵奧利佛逝世的母親。奧利佛打了諾亞，把他打倒在地上。夏綠蒂與索爾伯利太太都站在諾亞那一邊，一起痛打奧利佛。諾亞跑去叫來了邦柏先生，控訴奧利佛想要謀殺他跟夏綠蒂。接著，邦柏先生再度痛打奧利佛。

奧利佛知道自己無法忍受殯葬業的生活，第二天的黎明，他就收拾一些衣服逃走了。

奧利佛決定要走路去倫敦，他相信在那個大城市裡面，邦柏先生不會找到他。奧利佛靠著乞討活了下來。在第七天，他來到了一個叫做巴內特的小鎮，在那裡，一個很有自信的男孩來跟他打招呼，他自我介紹叫做傑克·道金斯，更響亮的名號叫做「狡猾的機靈鬼」。他給奧利佛帶來食物，並且帶他進入倫敦。他答應奧利佛可以在倫敦替他找到住的地方，那地方是由傑克的一個老朋友，一個可敬的「老紳士」所提供。

機靈鬼帶著奧利佛來到城市貧民區裡的廢棄房子，在一個極髒亂的樓上房間裡面，奧利佛遇到了費金，他是一個外表邪惡的老猶太人，長著一頭紅色的捲髮與一臉鬍子。那兒還有一群男孩子在抽菸斗和喝酒。房間裡面四處吊著大量的絲質手帕。

奧利佛那時並不知道，那些男孩偷來這些手帕讓費金拿去賣。兩個年輕的女人，南西與貝特來訪。她們也協助費金做事，但奧利佛年紀太小，不知道她們也是妓女。費金開始訓練奧利佛從他的口袋中拿走手帕，奧利佛以為這只是個遊戲。

一天，費金派奧利佛、機靈鬼與另外一個叫做查理‧貝茲的男孩子出去工作。他們駐足在一個老紳士的身後，這名老紳士正在書攤上閱讀一本書。機靈鬼從老紳士的口袋裡拿走了手帕，兩個男孩就跑掉了，可是奧利佛動作太慢，當這個老紳士看到奧利佛，大叫「抓賊！」一群人開始追逐奧利佛，然後奧利佛就被捕了。

在警察局裡，這名紳士，布朗洛先生，為這個無家可歸的小男孩感到難過。接著，書販來了，他作證說是另外一個男孩偷了手帕。布朗洛先生要離開這個地方時，看到奧利佛病懨懨地躺在地上，他叫了馬車，帶著奧利佛回到他家裡。在那裡，奧利佛受到良好的照顧與善心的對待，這是他出生後第一次受到這樣的待遇。

於此同時，機靈鬼與查理‧貝茲回到了費金的住所。這名老罪犯（費金）非常地生氣，因為警察知道了他們的惡行。他害怕奧利佛會把他們的地方供出來，就決定要把整個犯罪集團搬到另外一個房子去。

接著，費金計畫綁架奧利佛。當奧利佛出門為布朗洛先生辦事時，南西與她的男友，一個叫做比爾‧賽克斯的凶惡強盜抓住了奧利佛，並把他帶回去給費金。可是，南希覺得奧利佛很可憐，不讓賽克斯與費金毆打他。費金恐嚇奧利佛，讓他不敢再試圖逃跑。

費金說服賽克斯，讓奧利佛協助他搶劫一個鄉間的房子。賽克斯與其他兩名搶匪利用奧利佛爬進小窗子裡，要他從裡面為大門解鎖。可是，僕人們聽到了他們的聲音，擊發了手槍。奧利佛被傷到手臂。賽克斯拉著他逃跑，因為奧利佛傷得太重，賽克斯就把他丟在一條水溝裡。

回到倫敦，費金聽到搶劫失敗，他祕密地與一個叫做蒙克斯的人會面，告訴他這個消息。蒙克斯一直在找奧利佛。他一直付錢給費金，確保奧利佛會留下犯罪記錄，不過蒙克斯並沒有跟費金說為什麼。

在賽克斯離開之後，奧利佛失去了意識，躺在水溝裡。他醒來以後，蹣跚地走回那個房子，尋求幫助。那些僕人認出來他是盜賊的一員。然而，梅莉太太，也就是擁有這幢房子的老太太，對這小孩產生了同情心，並叫來家庭醫師替他治療。梅莉太太與她的養女，年輕美麗的蘿絲小姐，就這樣照顧著奧利佛。

奧利佛跟她們訴說自己的故事。因此，梅莉一家人就帶著奧利佛去倫敦尋找布朗洛先生。他們發現他已經離開倫敦前往西印度群島。於是他們帶著奧利佛回去，在一

個鄉下的小莊園快樂地生活。

在倫敦，費金找到賽克斯躲藏的地方並前去拜訪。南西正在照顧賽克斯。同時，蒙克斯來了。這個老罪犯（費金）把他帶到一個私人的房間，南西在門外偷聽，她聽到他們的對話，知道奧利佛有危險了。

南西知道梅莉一家正在倫敦，她想要拯救奧利佛，因此就偷偷地前往他們住的旅館。蘿絲小姐就在那兒，南西告訴她，蒙克斯就是奧利佛同父異母的兄弟，也因此非法繼承了父親所有的財產。她承諾每個禮拜天晚上十一點到十二點之間，會到倫敦橋上會見任何蘿絲小姐需要且可以為奧利佛的出身作證的人，並告訴他整個事情的來龍去脈。

蘿絲小姐知道布朗洛先生已經回到倫敦。她前去拜會他，跟他解釋奧利佛發生了什麼事情。布朗洛先生說他們必須見到南西，並且找到蒙克斯的藏身處。

南西告訴他們如何找到蒙克斯。可是，她被跟蹤了。費金產生了懷疑，找人跟蹤了這次的會面。南西拒絕了布朗洛先生為她安排安全的住所，她說自己還愛著賽克斯。

費金告訴賽克斯南西背叛了他們，事實上，她請求布朗洛先生答應只起訴蒙克斯。賽克斯在狂怒中毆打南西致死。接著他逃逸了，警察在追捕他。

布朗洛先生找到了蒙克斯，威脅說要揭露他的罪行，除非他把所有關於奧利佛的事情全盤托出。蒙克斯坦白說，他的父母婚姻並不快樂。蒙克斯的本名叫做愛德華‧立佛德。他的父親，艾德溫‧立佛德在與妻子分離後，就愛上了奧利佛的母親，安妮‧弗萊明。

然而，在艾德溫要娶安妮之前，安妮已經懷孕了，並且艾德溫也必須出差工作。他留下一紙遺言說，要是這個未出生的孩子沒有犯罪的話，就可以得到他一部分的財產。接著，他就生病去世了。這就是為什麼蒙克斯要讓奧利佛留下犯罪記錄。

蒙克斯告訴布朗洛說，安妮離家出走，因為她的未婚懷孕讓家人蒙羞。她來到了孩子父親墳墓的附近。她自己的父親也過世了，留下她的姊妹蘿絲孤苦伶仃，住在附近的梅莉太太同情蘿絲並收養了她。

最後，蒙克斯答應簽下一紙文件，讓奧利佛得到他的財產。賽克斯在一處廢棄的屋子裡被警察找到。他在使用一條繩子要跳下房子的時候，不小心把自己吊死了。費金被逮捕，判了死刑。他的幫派被抓去坐牢或是被外放到澳洲。蒙克斯離開了這個國家，幾年後死在美國的監獄裡。

布朗洛先生收養了奧利佛。他在梅莉一家附近的鄉間買了一幢房子，奧利佛終於可以開始他平靜的人生。

一、閱讀測驗 (Reading Comprehension)

答 1. C　　2. B　　3. A　　4. D

解析：

1. 由文章可以得知，本文主要是在描述奧利佛早年悲慘的生活，因此答案為 (C)。
2. 費金最後的下場是被逮捕而且被判了死刑，並不是被傑克·道金斯殺害，所以 (B) 的敘述不正確，為本題的答案。
3. 蒙克斯想要讓奧利佛留下犯罪記錄的原因，是因為不想讓奧利佛獲得一部分的遺產，因此答案為 (A)。
4. 由文中所描述的奧利佛所遭遇到的種種事情來判斷，可以推論出當時的社會普遍不重視人權，因此答案為 (D)。

二、字彙填充 (Fill in the Blanks)

答 1. exposed　　2. bullying　　3. compassion

三、引導式翻譯 (Guided Translation)

答 1. fell; in; love; with　　2. gave; birth; to　　3. too; to

Chapter 8
Jane Eyre

簡愛

　　簡愛自小就是個孤兒，她被送去與有錢的舅媽莎拉‧里德一起住。這女人自己有三名小孩子，兩名女孩與一名男孩，也就是簡的表兄妹。莎拉‧里德對自己的三名小孩寵愛有加，卻對簡非常殘酷而沒感情。在這三名表兄妹間，約翰常欺負簡。

　　有一天，約翰因為一本書與簡起了衝突。這男孩把書丟向簡，打中了她，讓她摔倒，她的頭撞到了門，流血了。「你這個邪惡殘酷的小孩！」簡大叫，那男孩衝向她，打了她一頓。簡被這男孩打得很慘，就很激烈地反擊，然後這男孩痛苦地大叫：「討厭的人！討厭的人！」

　　莎拉‧里德趕到兩人扭打的現場時，把簡抓去一個叫做紅屋的房間，這是一間讓簡害怕的房間，因為這是里德先生過世的地方。簡極度恐懼，也極度迷信，覺得自己見到舅舅的鬼魂，這讓她失去了意識。

　　在接受過一些治療之後，簡知道自己將要被送到羅伍德學院。在她要離開舅媽的宅第時，這家遠親裡沒有人來跟她道別。

　　簡發現羅伍德學院是一個很難適應的地方。這裡的老師非常嚴格，院長也非常小氣。這裡的女孩們常常又餓又冷，不過，簡在這裡得到了一個朋友，她叫做海倫‧伯恩斯。後來院裡流行起傷寒，很多的學生生病過世。她的朋友海倫也生病了，不過她得的病是肺結核。簡到海倫的房間陪伴她，可是在這兩名女孩睡夢之間，海倫過世了。

　　簡後來在羅伍德學院待了八年，念了六年的書，最後兩年執教。不過，簡一直渴望去看看外面的世界，因此，她登了一個廣告，應徵兒童家庭教師。有人回應了她的廣告。簡就在桑菲爾德莊園得到了家庭教師的位置，這是一個離羅伍德學院大約五十英里的宅第。

　　到達桑菲爾德莊園之後，簡見到了她的學生，一個叫做愛黛兒的法國小女孩。她也遇到了這幢宅第的主人，羅徹斯特先生，並與他墜入愛河。簡喜歡這份教導小孩的工作，但她對於有時會聽到宅第裡傳出神祕的叫聲與雜音感到疑惑。有一天晚上，簡被一個可怕的笑聲驚醒，她出去查探怎麼回事。她發現羅徹斯特先生的房間著火了，可是她沒辦法叫醒羅徹斯特先生，她撲滅了火，救了他的性命。

　　過了一些時候，簡走在桑菲爾德莊園的花園裡，羅徹斯特先生把她叫過來，他對簡坦白了自己的情意，並跟她求婚，簡非常驚訝，不敢置信，但最後還是接受了羅徹斯特先生的求婚。

桑菲爾德莊園裡都在準備著羅徹斯特先生與簡的婚禮。一天晚上，一個瘋狂的女人來到簡的房間，把她結婚用的頭紗撕成兩半。簡跟羅徹斯特先生說了這件事，羅徹斯特先生就在婚禮前安排簡住在不同的房間。

　　就在羅徹斯特先生與簡於教堂交換誓言時，一個聲音抗議羅徹斯特先生的婚約，這聲音來自梅森先生，他說羅徹斯特先生已經結婚了。在羅徹斯特先生年輕的時候，就在牙買加與一個女人結婚了，而這女人已經發瘋。原來這個叫做柏莎的女人，一直都被藏在宅第三樓。所以簡聽到的叫聲就是來自於柏莎，是她放火燒了羅徹斯特先生的房間，而且也是她將簡的頭紗撕成兩半。

　　知道這些事情之後，簡非常地沮喪。羅徹斯特先生想要與她一起逃到法國去，這個決定更讓她痛不欲生。她最後決定不想變成羅徹斯特先生的情婦，就帶著自己僅有的財物，在半夜逃出了桑菲爾德莊園。

　　簡搭上了一輛馬車，用身上的錢盡量去到最遠的地方。在下馬車的時候，她不小心把其他財物放在車上。身無分文的狀況之下，簡在夜晚被迫睡在屋外。第二天，她來到一個小鎮，在一家麵包店，她想用自己的手帕與手套換取東西吃。店裡的女人拒絕了她，簡只好繼續往前走。在一個農莊，她看到一個農夫在吃麵包與起士，簡向他乞討一些食物，他就切給她厚厚一片麵包。

　　簡繼續往前走，最後來到了一個房子前，這裡住著兩位女士、一位男士與一個女傭。當她敲門的時候，女傭要她離開，並且關上了門。簡虛弱地倒在地上，在那時，她聽到了一個聲音，這是聖約翰‧里佛斯先生的聲音。他讓簡進到房子裡來，他之前一直在聽簡與僕人的對話。

　　簡在里佛斯這裡住了一段時間，最後她發現自己與這家人有血緣關係，他們是她的表親。簡也知道她那過世的叔叔留給她一筆很大的遺產。為了表示謝意，簡決定要將遺產均分給自己新獲得的家人。

　　聖約翰‧里佛斯決定要前往印度傳教。可是，他想要簡嫁給他，並跟他一起去。簡仍然非常愛著羅徹斯特先生，並向聖約翰表明他們倆無法像一對夫婦一樣相愛。

　　聖約翰‧里佛斯沒有停止追求簡，他延後了自己的印度之行，他告訴簡要是她不聽從自己的想法，就是違背主的意思。接著他就對簡非常嚴厲，讓簡對他產生了恨意。

　　一天傍晚，在晚餐之前，聖約翰‧里佛斯說了一篇禱文，言詞感動了簡。簡知道他很有演說家的天分，然後就開始懷疑自己。她在想，自己是否能夠妥協，嫁給聖約翰，跟他一起去印度。在這時候，她身體裡出現一個奇怪的感覺。她的心跳加速，聖約翰問她怎麼了。在這時候，簡聽到了羅徹斯特先生的聲音說著：「簡！簡！簡！」

　　第二天，簡搭上一輛馬車，回到桑菲爾德莊園。抵達的時候，她從馬車車站走了兩英里的路前往宅第。簡發現整個宅第都成了廢墟，窗戶都破了，屋頂也倒塌了。石

頭都變成黑色，顯示這裡曾經發生過可怕的大火。這裡一個人都沒有，所以簡離開了，前往附近的城鎮了解發生了什麼事。

在一間叫做羅徹斯特·阿姆斯的旅館裡，簡向一名男人詢問了關於桑菲爾德莊園的事情。他說那個叫做柏莎的女人引起了這場火。羅徹斯特先生救了僕人，也試著要救柏莎，那時她已經跑上了屋頂。羅徹斯特先生呼喊著柏莎的名字，可是她跳下來結束了自己的性命。雖然羅徹斯特先生在這場大火中活下來，但他失去了自己的手與視力。旅館裡的男人接著告訴簡，羅徹斯特先生住在一個叫做芬迪恩的宅第裡，那是在三十英里外的一處荒涼之地。

簡立刻前往芬迪恩。那是一個藏在樹林深處的老建築，羅徹斯特先生與兩名僕人，約翰與瑪麗，就住在那裡。當簡抵達那邊的時候，已經很晚了。她看到了羅徹斯特先生就在裡面，她覺得他看起來就像以前一樣，只是臉上總有一股哀傷與寂寞。

簡敲了敲門，瑪麗來應門。她看到簡時感到非常驚訝，這僕人正要拿一個有蠟燭與水的托盤給羅徹斯特先生。簡從僕人那接過托盤，帶去給羅徹斯特先生。當她進到房間裡時，羅徹斯特的狗，派洛特，聽到了簡的聲音，就很開心地跑向她，害簡差點摔了托盤。當她要這隻狗趴下來時，羅徹斯特先生聽到了她的聲音，以為自己在做夢。當他知道自己不是在做夢時，就緊緊地抱住了簡。

羅徹斯特先生感謝上帝把簡帶回他的身邊。他們彌補了彼此的關係，並在一個安靜的小教堂結婚。在故事要結束的時候，簡述說著她已經過了十年的快樂婚姻生活。羅徹斯特先生經歷了兩年的盲眼生活之後，也開始恢復視力。他可以用一隻眼睛看到東西了，也可以看到他們的第一個兒子出生。

答案

一、閱讀測驗 (Reading Comprehension)

答 1. B　　2. C　　3. D　　4. A

解析：

1. 海倫確實是簡的好朋友，但是後來罹患結核病而過世，簡後來是自己一個人到桑菲爾德莊園去當家庭教師，因此 (B) 的敘述是錯誤的，為本題的答案。

2. 當聖約翰·里佛斯向簡求婚時，她覺得自己仍然愛著羅徹斯特先生，因此並沒有答應求婚，故正確答案為 (C)。

3. 在簡離開桑菲爾德莊園之後，柏莎放火燒了羅徹斯特先生的莊園宅第，而羅徹斯特先生雖然在火災中倖存下來，但也失去一隻手和視力，因此可以說是受了重

傷，故正確答案為 (D)。

4. 綜觀全文，簡雖然遇到許多困境，但是她都沒有因此而屈服於命運，反而是不斷地挺身對抗命運、為自己找到出路，因此可以推知她是一位很堅強的女性，不輕易向命運屈服，故正確答案為 (A)。

二、字彙填充 (Fill in the Blanks)

答 1. evidence   2. stingy   3. collapsed

三、引導式翻譯 (Guided Translation)

答 1. longs; to; become   2. belong; to   3. put; off

精選 8 回經典英國文學名著，帶你遊歷文學的時光之旅！

英國文學起源甚早，本書呈現了古英文時期、文藝復興時期、十八世紀和十九世紀中葉等不同時期的英國文學作品，反映作家的所思所慮，以及所處時代的價值觀。

透過 8 篇經典的文學作品，帶你在閱讀之後，能領略作者的所思所慮，以及所處時代的價值觀。並透過文本引出各項與人生息息相關的議題。文學關懷人生，書寫人生的百態！藉由精挑細選的文學名著，讓你探索人性、擴大自我的視野，同時提升英文閱讀力！

★ 精選 8 篇經典英國文學作品，囊括各類議題，如性別平等、人權、海洋教育等。
★ 獨家收錄故事背景的知識補充。
★ 附精闢賞析、文章中譯及電子朗讀音檔，讓你自學也能輕鬆讀懂文學作品。
★ 可搭配 108 課綱英文多元選修及加深加廣選修課程。

三民網路書店
www.sanmin.com.tw

「閱讀經典文學時光之旅：英國篇」與「解析本」不分售
80715G